I0649230

William Henry Rideing, William H. (William Henry) Rideing

The boyhood of famous authors

William Henry Rideing, William H. (William Henry) Rideing

The boyhood of famous authors

ISBN/EAN: 9783337374006

Printed in Europe, USA, Canada, Australia, Japan

Cover: Foto ©Raphael Reischuk / pixelio.de

More available books at **www.hansebooks.com**

THE BOYHOOD

OF

FAMOUS AUTHORS

BY

WILLIAM H. RIDEING

AUTHOR OF "THACKERAY'S LONDON," ETC.

" The spirit of a youth
That means to be of note."
SHAKESPEARE

NEW YORK: 46 EAST FOURTEENTH STREET
THOMAS Y. CROWELL & COMPANY
BOSTON: 100 PURCHASE STREET

PREFACE.

——— · · ———

THIS little book having run entirely out
of print, a new edition has been prepared,
which it is believed will be found more
attractive than the earlier ones. Some of
the authors represented in the first edition having passed away (Holmes, Lowell,
Whittier, and Boyesen), the title has been
changed from " The Boyhood of Living
Authors " to the more comprehensive one
of " The Boyhood of Famous Authors."
New chapters on Robert Louis Stevenson
and Rudyard Kipling have been substituted for others deemed less interesting;
and portraits of the authors, together with
their autographs in the form of original
letters or extracts from their works, have
been added to the embellishments. What
was said in the preface to the first edition

may be repeated now : Every chapter has
been prepared with the approval, and in
most cases with the assistance, of the authors represented, and may therefore be
taken as entirely trustworthy.

WILLIAM H. RIDEING.

CONTENTS.

BOYHOOD OF FAMOUS AUTHORS.

OLIVER WENDELL HOLMES.

THERE is a pleasant little house in Beacon Street, Boston, which is occupied by a gentleman who has written some books which have made his name famous wherever the English language is spoken, and also in many other countries into the language of which they have been translated. As he goes along the streets of the town, with a friendly, observant eye, which has a bird-like quickness, people who see him whisper — those who are unmannered point at him — and say, " See, the Autocrat ! "

He is probably referred to thus as often as by his proper name ; and this is because one of his books is called " The Autocrat of the Breakfast Table," a volume full of wisdom and humor, which on one page moves us to tears, and in the next sets us shaking with laughter. He is a rather slender gentleman, with white hair, though no one would guess him to be over seventy-five; and the wavy white hair on his head is matched by white side-whiskers of an English cut. He is not distinctly a writer for the young; writing of any kind has not been the business of his life, indeed, and aside from it he has made himself famous in the medical profession : but there are few boys or girls who, though they may not have read "The Autocrat of the Breakfast Table" all through, do not know by heart "The Chambered Nautilus" and the story of the deacon's "One-hoss Shay."

> "Have you heard of the wonderful one-hoss shay
> That was built in such a logical way?
> It ran a hundred years to a day,
> And then, of a sudden, it —   Ah, but stay !
> I'll tell you what happened without delay ;
> Scaring the parson into fits,
> Frightening people out of their wits, —
> Have you heard of that, I say?"

296 Beacon St

Oct. 28th 1887

Dear Mr. Riding,

I am greatly pleased
with the picture where I am
shown in the seat by the rock.

That with the tree is
good, but the water and
the island (Great Misery) are
rather indistinct.

The other, (where I am rather
standing) is not to my mind—
It makes one too chalky for
a living creature.

With many thanks I accept
my copies and return yours.

Yours very truly

O. W. Holmes.

It is Dr. Oliver Wendell Holmes I am speaking about; one of the two survivors of that splendid period of American literature which gave us Longfellow, Motley, Emerson, and Lowell.

The doctor's study in the house in Beacon Street looks out over the Charles River; and it is a question whether the view from the windows is more beautiful at night, when the electric lights on the bridge cast their reflections on the water like javelins of glittering silver, or in the day, when the gray stream flowing to the sea, and the spires and towers of Cambridge, with the green hills of Arlington and Belmont beyond, are visible. It is at all times a view of which Boston people are very proud; and, aside from its beauty, it has the added interest to the doctor of encompassing nearly all the scenes of his youth, and of his manhood too.

He was born at Cambridge, and went to school at Cambridgeport, and both of those places are in sight from his windows. All his past is unfolded there; and when he turns from the book or manuscript on his

desk, near which hangs the portrait of
his renowned ancestress, " Dorothy Q.,"
he can see the paths his feet have followed
since the beginning.

He can see himself at various ages : the
urchin straggling to school, through fields
which are green only in the memory now ;
the Harvard student ; and then, in one
person, the college professor and the famous author. No doubt he finds it hard
to believe that the urchin was not another
fellow altogether, instead of the self-same
sapling that he himself once was ; but,
though the identity is confusing, he can
remember the boy well, and all his queer
fancies, amusements, and chums.

A moderately studious boy he was, fond
of reading stories, especially " The Arabian
Nights ; " fond of whispering, and whittling,
as his desk showed ; a little mischievous ;
sound in mind and in body, but more than
usually imaginative. " No Roman sooth-
sayer," he says in one of his books, " ever
had such a catalogue of omens as I found
in the sibylline leaves of my childhood.
That trick of throwing a stone at a tree.

and attaching some mighty issue to hitting
or missing, which you will find mentioned
in one or more biographies, I well remember. Stepping on or over certain particular things, — Dr. Johnson's especial
weakness, — I got the habit of at a very
early age.

"With these follies mingled sweet delu-
sions, which I loved so well I would not
outgrow them, even when it required a
voluntary effort to put a momentary trust
in them. Here is one I cannot help telling
you : —

"The firing of the great guns at the
Navy-Yard is easily heard at the place
where I was born and lived. 'There is a
ship of war come in,' they used to say when
they heard them. Of course, I supposed
that such vessels came in unexpectedly,
after indefinite years of absence, — suddenly as fallen stones, — and that the
great guns roared in their astonishment
and delight at the sight of the old war-
ship splitting the bay with her cut-water.
Now, the sloop-of-war the 'Wasp,' Capt.
Blakely, after gloriously capturing the

'Reindeer' and the 'Avon,' had disappeared from the face of the ocean, and was supposed to be lost. But there was no proof of it, and of course, for a time, hopes were entertained that she might be heard from. Long after the last chance had utterly vanished, I pleased myself with the fond illusion that somewhere on the waste of waters she was still floating; and there were *years* during which I never heard the sound of the great guns booming inland from the Navy-Yard without saying to myself, 'The " Wasp " has come! ' and almost thinking I could see her, as she rolled in, crumpling the water before her, weather-beaten, barnacled, with shattered spars and threadbare canvas, welcomed by the shouts and tears of thousands.

" This was one of the dreams that I nursed and never told. Let me make a clean breast of it now, and say, that so late as to have outgrown childhood, perhaps to have got far on to manhood, when the roar of the cannon has struck suddenly on my ear, I have started with a thrill of vague expectation and tremulous delight, and the

long-unspoken words have articulated themselves in the mind's dumb whisper, ' The
" Wasp " has come ! ' "

Dr. Holmes was born on the 29th of
August, 1809, and one of the earliest things
he can remember is giving three cheers for
the close of the war of 1812. Until about
two years ago, when it was pulled down,
his birthplace stood on the edge of the
college grounds at Cambridge ; and the old
" gambrel-roofed " house was one of the
sights of the town which visitors seldom
missed.

> " ' Gambrel ! gambrel ! ' — Let me beg
> You'll look at a horse's hinder leg, —
> First great angle above the hoof, —
> That's the gambrel : hence gambrel-roof."

It had been the headquarters of the
American army during the siege of Boston ;
and when Oliver Wendell was born, it was
the parsonage of his father, who was pastor
of the First Church. A rambling, roomy
old house it was, with untenanted upper
chambers that were always locked, and a
garret where strange noises could be heard,

— the very place, in the imagination of a little boy, for ghosts and creatures from fairy-land. Then there was a dark store-room ; and peeping through the keyhole he could see heaps of chairs and tables, and he fancied that somehow they had rushed in there frightened, and had huddled together and climbed upon each other's backs for protection. Sometimes he thought he could hear the swords and spurs of soldiers clanking in the passages ; and the floor of his father's study was covered with dents left by the butts of the muskets of the armed men who had used it as a council-chamber.

Upstairs there was the portrait of a lady, with sword-thrusts through it, — marks of the British officers' rapiers, — and this is the same picture that now hangs on the wall of the library in Beacon Street.

> On her hand a parrot green
> Sits unmoving, and broods serene.
> Hold up the canvas full in view —
> Look, there's a rent the light shines through !
> Dark with a century's fringe of dust,
> That was a Red-coat's rapier thrust."

Who has not heard of that picture of
Dorothy Quincy, or, as she is familiarly
called Dorothy Q., the Autocrat's great-
grandmother? His musical verses have
engraved it in the minds of thousands who
never saw it, or even a reproduction of it.

Cambridge was then a country village,
and it was a pleasant walk through fields
and lanes to the school in Cambridgeport,
to which Oliver Wendell was sent when he
was scarcely out of his infancy, — pleasant
when he had company; but he had more
than his share of childish fancies, and on
his way there was a great wooden hand —
a glove-maker's sign — which used to
swing and creak, and fill him with terror.

" Oh, the dreadful hand !" he says in
one of his essays, " always hanging there
ready to catch up a little boy who would
come home to supper no more, nor get to
bed, — whose porringer would be laid away
empty thenceforth, and his half-worn shoes
wait until his smaller brother grew to fit
them ! "

Then there were encounters with the
" Port-chucks," — as the Cambridge boys

called the boys of Cambridgeport, — and any new article of dress was sure to be criticised by these young Philistines. One morning Oliver Wendell had on a new hat of Leghorn straw.

" Hullo, you-sir," said a " Port-chuck," " yoo know th' wuz gon-to be a race to-morrah ? "

" No," replied Oliver innocently. " Who's gon-to run, 'n' where 's 't gon-to be ? "

" Squire Mico 'n' Doctor Williams, round the brim o' your hat."

The " Port-chuck " put his tongue into his cheek, and Oliver saw that he had been trifled with.

The school was kept by a stout old lady, called Dame Prentiss, who ruled the children with a long willow rod, which reached across the room. It was used for reminding rather than for chastising, however ; and when one rod gave out, the scholars had no hesitation in providing her with a new one, which they went into the fields for themselves. Now and then a ferule was the instrument of punishment ; and on one occasion, when Oliver had been caught whittling his desk, the dame brought it down across his hand with startling results: it fell into pieces as it touched his palm, though this was probably due to a flaw in the material of the ferule rather than to the toughness of the boy.

When he had outgrown petticoats, he went to other schools in Cambridgeport; and he had among his schoolmates Alfred Lee, who afterwards became Bishop of Delaware; Margaret Fuller; and Richard Henry Dana, the author of that fascinating sea-story, "Two Years Before the Mast."

So far he had always lived in the old home with the gambrel roof, which had been growing dearer and dearer to him; but at the age of fifteen he entered the Phillips Academy at Andover, and then for the first time he felt the pangs of home-sickness. His year there was not very happy.

"The clock was dreadfully slow in striking the hour when recess began, and the professors looked as if they were always thinking of death," he said to the writer of this sketch not long ago.

But he had pleasant memories of Andover, too; and in 1878, when the academy was a century old, he went back and read a beautiful poem describing the sensations with which he entered it : —

"The morning came : I reached the classic hall ;
A clock-face eyed me staring from the wall ;
Beneath its hands a printed line I read : —
YOUTH IS LIFE'S SEED-TIME ; so the clock-face said.
Some took its counsel, as the sequel showed —
Sowed — their wild oats, and reaped as they had
    sowed.

" How all comes back ! the upward slanting floor ;
The masters' thrones that flank the central door ;
The long outstretching alleys that divide
The rows of desks that stand on either side ;
The staring boys, a face to every desk,
Bright, dull, pale, blooming, common, picturesque.

" Grave is the Master's look ; his forehead wears
Thick rows of wrinkles, fruits of worrying cares ;
Uneasy lie the heads of all that rule, —
His most of all whose kingdom is a school.
Supreme he sits ; before the awful frown
That bends his brows, the boldest eye goes down ;
Not more submissive Israel heard and saw
At Sinai's foot the Giver of the Law."

After a year at Andover, Oliver Wendell
entered Harvard University; and while he
was there, he maintained a fair rank for
scholarship. Then he studied law for a
year; and after that he chose what was to
be the occupation of his life, — the study
and practice of medicine.

His literary gifts were already known.
When he was about twenty-one, the old
frigate "Constitution," or the "Old Iron-
sides" as she was called, lay in the Charles-
town Navy-Yard, and the Government
proposed to break her up. Some stirring
lines protesting against her destruction appeared in "The Boston Advertiser," from
which they were copied by other newspapers, and then circulated on printed slips.
They aroused such enthusiasm in favor of
the old ship, that the Government con-
sented to her preservation, and the author
found his name on every lip : it was Oliver
Wendell Holmes.   Other verses, including
"The Height of the Ridiculous," came from
the same pen, which were no less popular ;
and the young poet had encouragement
enough to leave the laboratory, and devote

himself to the quill. But he remembered,
no doubt, what a wise man once said about
literature as a profession : it is a good
walking-stick, but a poor crutch. He continued to be a doctor, and rose to eminence
as a professor in the Harvard Medical
School ; but in his spare hours he culti-
vated the genius which is as radiant as a
star in his books.

THE HEIGHT OF THE RIDICULOUS.

BY OLIVER WENDELL HOLMES.

I wrote some lines once on a time,
  In wondrous merry mood,
And thought, as usual, men would say
  They were exceeding good.

They were so queer, so very queer,
  I laughed as I would die :
Albeit, in the general way,
  A sober man am I.

I called my servant, and he came :
  How kind it was of him
To mind a slender man like me,
  He of the mighty limb !

"These to the printer!" I exclaimed,
  And in my humorous way
I added (as a trifling jest),
  "There'll be the devil to pay."

He took the paper, and I watched,
  And saw him peep within :
At the first line he read, his face
  Was all upon the grin.

He read the next : the grin grew broad,
  And shot from ear to ear ;
He read the third : a chuckling noise
  I now began to hear.

The fourth : he broke into a roar ;
  The fifth : his waistband split ;
The sixth : he burst five buttons off,
  And tumbled in a fit.

Ten days and nights, with sleepless eyes
  I watched that wretched man :
And since, I never dare to write
  As funny as I can.

THOMAS BAILEY ALDRICH.

A GOOD many years ago now, a small bare-legged boy set out from his home in Portsmouth, N.H., for an afternoon's sport with a gun. He rambled along, as boys will, with his eyes wide open for every thing that came under them, as well as for the game that was the special object of his expedition; and he had not gone far when he saw a chaise approaching, driven by the Governor of the State.

The Governor was a very popular and distinguished man, who was being talked of for the Presidency; and we should not have liked the small boy if he had not been a little overawed by finding himself alone in the presence of so august a personage. He was equal to the occasion, however; and as the chaise reached him, he stood aside to let it pass, and gravely presented arms. The Governor at once pulled up his

EDITORIAL OFFICE OF
The Atlantic Monthly,
BOSTON.

June 13th /85

Dear Ridving:

I shall try to be on hand when you tip up that horn of plenty

I can't do anything with Carpenter question, which is quite striking, in conclusion I'm more vexed than I can place.

In haste
Ever yours,
S. B. Aldrich

horse, and looked with amusement at the little fellow standing there as serious as a sentry, with his gun held rigidly before him.

"What is your name?" said the Governor.

"Thomas Bailey Aldrich," replied the boy, with a military salute.

He was invited into the chaise; and. though he lost his shooting, what was that in comparison with the distinction of riding into Portsmouth Town with Governor Woodbury?

This was forty years ago, and since then Thomas Bailey Aldrich has earned a place among the foremost of American authors by a series of books, some in prose and some in verse, which are distinguished by the purity of their tone, the refinement of their style, and the picturesqueness of their invention. One of them is called "The Story of a Bad Boy;" and except that some of the names of persons and places are changed, it is so faithful a picture of the author's boyhood that it might be called an autobiography. If any one has not read that book, I advise him to do so at once;

and when he has finished it, he will, I think,
be ready to thank me for introducing it to
him.

" Not such a very bad boy, but a pretty
bad boy," the author says of himself. A
pretty good boy we should call him, — a
boy who would do nothing mean, cruel, or
vulgar, though he was as ready for mischief
as any of his playfellows.

One cannot imagine a better place than
Portsmouth for the bringing up of such a
boy. It is a romantic old town by the sea,
full of quaint old homesteads. It is built
at the mouth of the Piscataqua River, and
may be said to have been founded by Capt.
John Smith, the famous adventurer, who,
after slaying Turks in hand-to-hand com-
bats, and doing all sorts of doughty deeds in
various parts of the globe, visited the coast
of New Hampshire in 1612, and recommended this as the site of a future seaport.

Time was when Portsmouth carried on a
great trade with the West Indies, and
threatened to eclipse both Boston and New
York; it turned out the best ships and the
smartest sailors, and in the war of 1812 it

equipped many a daring privateer. But its prosperity slipped away from it ; and all the old wharves are now deserted, though when the sun shines upon them it brings out a vague perfume of the cargoes of rum, molasses, and spice, that used to be piled upon them.

What boy wandering along wharves like these, and hearing from superannuated sailors of the former glories of the place, would not long to go to sea ? There were few boys in Rivermouth, as it is called in " The Story of a Bad Boy," who had not this ambition ; and early in life Aldrich began the study of navigation, though he was not destined to use his knowledge in picking paths across the sea by the aid of the sun and stars.

The wharves were not the only stimulus to the spirit of romance in this old town. In the shady streets were historic houses in which Washington, Lafayette, and the King of the French had been entertained ; the ghosts of former greatness seemed to haunt them ; dark wainscot stood high against the walls ; strange carvings with

winged heads clustered about the doors;
shadowy portraits of bewigged gentlemen
and furbelowed dames, each with some
legend attached to it,hung from the mould-
ings; and winding stairways led into mys-
terious chambers under the roofs. It seems
to me that an imaginative boy brought up
amid such surroundings was bound to
become either a sailor or an author, — that
he would either yield to the fascinations of
the wharves, and go to sea, or stay ashore
to write the stories and the poems which
would be sure to come into his head in
the presence of these relics of an historic
past.

In one of those old houses which still
stand in Court Street, where it is now used
as a hospital, Aldrich was born, just forty-
nine years ago; that is, in 1837.   His
father was a merchant and banker who had
opened a business in New Orleans; and
it was the custom of his parents to keep
the boy, who was their only child, with
them in the South during the winter, and
to send him back to Portsmouth for the
summer.   These visits were continued

until he reached the age of thirteen, when he returned to Portsmouth to remain there for several years; and it was in this old town that all which was most memorable in his boyhood occurred.

He was a rather slender little fellow, but sound and vigorous, and ever ready for either sport or mischief. As many mishaps befell him as usually fall to the lot of a high-spirited and adventurous boy. He could defend himself from imposition, and he was expert in the various games which occupied his comrades. He was not a prodigy in any way; not marvellous either for his scholarship or his promise of future distinction. But he was very fond of reading, and spent many hours in a delightful old attic, where he found a lot of old books, among others being "Robinson Crusoe," "Baron Trenck," "Don Quixote," "The Arabian Nights," Defoe's "History of the Plague in London," and "Tristram Shandy." Of all these, Defoe's "History of the Plague" was his favorite.

Like all attics in old New - England houses, this one was the receptacle of all kinds of rubbish. "They never throw any thing away in New England," Aldrich said to me one day: "they always put it up in the attic." And here were cast-off clothing, legless chairs, crazy tables, and all sorts of things which time, and changes in fashions, had rendered useless.

Among the rest was an old hide-covered trunk; and seeing how little hair was left on it, Thomas Bailey thought he would attempt to restore it. He had seen in the window of a barber's shop a preparation which was highly recommended as a sure cure for baldness; and he purchased a bottle of this, and carefully applied it to the trunk. Then he went up stairs from day to day to watch the effect, but the result was not satisfactory; the trunk remained as bald as ever, and Thomas Bailey felt that he had wasted his money.

The first school he went to was Dame Bagley's; and from what he has told me of her, I shall always think of her as a character who ought to have belonged to one of Hawthorne's romances. She was a severe and angular person, who had a

peculiar method of punishing her pupils.
She constantly wore on the second finger
of her right hand an uncommonly heavy
thimble, and with this she would sharply
rap the offender on the head. "Thomas
Bailey, come here!" Tap, tap, tap, tap!
It does not seem like a severe penalty;
but she brought her finger down with such
force, that the culprit often felt that it was
going right through him.

The boy was not very happy with Dame
Bagley, whose school was a dreary, uncom-
fortable place. The yard was bricked, and
just one brick had been lifted out to allow
a solitary cucumber-vine to spring up; this
was what Dame Bagley would probably
have called "a richly-wooded landscape."
And then the benches in the schoolroom
were too high for his legs. His feet could
not reach the floor, and his back would
grow so tired that sometimes he threw
himself backward upon the floor in sheer
desperation.

It was an altogether pleasant change
when he left Dame Bagley's, and became
enrolled as a pupil at the Temple School.

The Temple School is constantly referred to in "The Story of a Bad Boy" as the Temple Grammar School, and nearly every thing which relates to the latter is true of the former; so that the reader can get a better idea of Aldrich's boyhood from that book than I can give him here. The mad pranks of the boys when he was initiated as a member of the Rivermouth Centi-pedes; the fight on Slatter's Hill, that Gettysburg of snowballs; the burning of the stage-coach, — all the adventures were described from real life. There is a won-derful pony in the book, and the pony is from real life too. According to the story, the Temple Grammar School was burned down one Fourth of July by a fire-cracker that flew in through a window. This was fiction at the time the book was published; but five years afterward, as if to make the chronicle veracious in every particular, the school was burned in just that way.

To my mind, one of the earliest signs Aldrich gave of his literary bent was his distaste for figures; arithmetic staggered him, and he confesses that he often had to seek help from his school-fellows. This was very wrong, of course; and the only excuse I can think of may not be regarded as an excuse at all, but rather as an aggravation of the offence. In return for the help he received in arithmetic, he revised the compositions of the class, and even went so far as entirely to write the essays of the boys who, though clever enough at figures, had no talent for literary exercises.

Before he reached the age of twelve, he had written a story called "Colenzo." It was about pirates and buccaneers, and the scene was on a tropical island, which was supposed to lie somewhere out at sea, about seven miles from Portsmouth. Then he wrote articles for one of the local papers; and to these utterances of precocious wisdom he signed the *nom de plume*, "Experience."

At sixteen, his school days came to an end; and, his father having died, he was sent to New York to become a clerk in his uncle's office. But day-books and ledgers had no more charm for him than elementary arithmetic; and by the time he reached twenty, he had broken loose from the counting-room, and won a recognized place for himself among the most original of American authors. Fourteen books now stand to his credit, — stories that linger in the mind like memories of sunny days, and poems that have the polish and brilliance of diamonds. Portsmouth, sometimes with its own name, sometimes as Rivermouth, is revived again and again in them; and in some charming verses he has celebrated his days on the Piscataqua, which were among the happiest, no doubt, that he has ever seen.

PISCATAQUA RIVER.

BY THOMAS BAILEY ALDRICH.

Thou singest by the gleaming isles,
  By woods, and fields of corn, —
Thou singest, and the sunlight smiles
  Upon my birthday morn.

But I within a city, I,
  So full of vague unrest,
Would almost give my life to lie
  An hour upon thy breast!

To let the wherry listless go,
  And, wrapt in dreamy joy,
Dip, and surge idly to and fro,
  Like the red harbor-buoy;

To sit in happy indolence,
  To rest upon the oars,
And catch the heavy earthy scents
  That blow from summer shores;

To see the rounded sun go down,
  And with its parting fires
Light up the windows of the town,
  And burn the tapering spires;

And then to hear the muffled tolls
  From steeples slim and white,
And watch, among the Isles of Shoals,
  The Beacon's orange light.

O River! flowing to the main
  Through woods, and fields of corn,
Hear thou my longing and my pain,
  This sunny birthday morn;

And take this song which sorrow shapes
  To music like thine own,
And sing it to the cliffs and capes
  And crags where I am known!

JOHN TOWNSEND TROWBRIDGE.

IF any one has succeeded in representing the average American boy in fiction, it is Mr. Trowbridge. The boys in some books we know of are so unreal that it does not seem possible that the author has ever been a boy himself; they are either milksops or juvenile Munchausens. But all of Mr. Trowbridge's boys give us the effect of having been photographed from life, and their actions are as natural as their characters.

He does not picture them in marvellous exploits on the Cordilleras, or beating the record of Hall and Kane in the Arctic regions, or doing what no boys probably ever did, except in the imagination. They are shrewd, active, hard-working fellows, on the farm or in the country store, and their struggles and adventures are just of that kind which American boys go through

To see the future flushed with morning fire,
  Rosy with banners, bright with listening spires,
Fresh fields inviting courage and desire,
  This is the glory of our youthful years!

John Townsend Trowbridge

everywhere. A good reason for this fidelity to nature is that Mr. Trowbridge himself was a typical American boy, and the experiences of his own youth are reflected in those of his characters.

> " My hands were filled with common tasks,
> My head with rare romances," —

he says in one of his poems. He was familiar in his boyhood with the labor of the field, the drudgery of the farm, the contentions of the district school, and those aspirations which carry a boy up stairs, when his day's work is done, to study by a rush-light or a cracked lamp in a cold garret.

" Some of the Jack Hazard stories, especially 'Jack,' 'A Chance for Himself,' and ' Doing His Best,' contain very faithful descriptions of the farm life and scenes in which I was brought up," he said to me one day. " Although you will not find much of me personally in those stories, the kind of school I sometimes went to is exactly pictured in 'Doing His Best;'

and ' Peach Hill Farm,' where so much of
the action takes place, was merely a fancy
name for my father's farm in Ogden."

His account of his boyhood is quite as
interesting as his stories, and I shall repeat
it here in almost the very words he used in
giving it to me.

His father was a farmer who in 1811
emigrated from the East to the wilderness
of Western New York, making the journey in winter with a young wife, a little
load of household goods, and an ox-team.
Western New York was then a wilderness
indeed. There was only one house where
the city of Rochester now stands; and
crossing the Genesee River on the ice, the
pioneer settled eight miles beyond, cut
·down the trees, built a log house, and made
a little farm in the woods.

In this log house a boy was born in the
winter of 1827 ; and to him was given the
name of John Townsend Trowbridge, John
Townsend having been a benefactor of the
father. He was not the first born, but
the eighth of nine children, and it is easy
to understand that there was no silver

spoon for him. He lived the ordinary life of farm boys in that region, and went to school six or seven months of the year until he was about fourteen, after which time he went only during the winter term, and worked on the farm all summer.

Neither silver spoons, nor any other luxuries, were there. But his mother was a woman of a refined and devotional nature ; and despite the load of care, his father was a cheerful man, a good musician, and a capital story-teller, who, when his stock of bear and panther stories had been exhausted, would sometimes amuse his children by talking to them in rhyme. There were books in the house, too ; and in reading them the boy escaped the poverty of his surroundings, and was borne in imagination into the wonderland of the poets and romancers.

" I took up the study of French by myself under peculiar disadvantages, having none of the books which now render the acquisition of that language so easy ; and learned to read and translate it in the chimney-corner, before I ever saw a person

who was at all conversant with it," he tells
us. Then he learned German and Latin in
the same way and under the same disadvantages.

A boy who had spirit enough for this
was sure to have ambitions ; and as he read
Scott, Byron, and Moore, he had an inex-
tinguishable desire to write. Though he
was vigorous, and fond of out-door sports,
he was shy and reticent, and he never
whispered his dreams even to his most intimate friend. But while he followed the
plough he planned romances and com-
posed verses, and at the end of the day
stole into some quiet place and wrote
them out.

This was the period in which he made
his acquaintance with Moore's poem
" Lalla Rookh ; " and he has described it
in some verses, from which we have already
quoted a line or two.

> " My hands were filled with common tasks,
>   My head with rare romances ;
> My old straw hat was bursting out
>   With light locks and bright fancies.

"In field or wood, my thoughts threw off
  The old prosaic trammels :
'The sheep were grazing antelopes,
  The cows, a train of camels.

"Under the shady apple-boughs,
  The book was my companion ;
And while I read, the orchard spread
  One mighty branching banyan.

"To mango-trees or almond groves,
  Were changed the plums and quinces ;
I was the poet Feramorz,
  And had, of course, my Princess.

"The well-curb was her canopied
  Rich palanquin ; at twilight,
'Twas her pavilion overhead,
  And not my garret skylight.

"Ah, Lalla Rookh ! O charmèd book !
  First love, in manhood slighted ;
To-day we rarely turn the page
  In which our youth delighted."

When he was sixteen years old his father
died ; and a year later he went to Illinois,
where he had a sister living in DuPage
County. The following winter he taught a
school in the neighborhood ; and then he

tried farming, though he had no taste for it.
He spent more time in shooting grouse
and hunting deer than in looking after his
land ; and his crop was a failure, though not
through any fault of his.   His heart was
set on authorship, and nothing else would
satisfy him.   Essays and poems were de-
spatched now and then to country papers,
and he tasted the   never-to-be-forgotten
ecstasy of seeing his name in print.

The general who has been victorious in
battle, the astronomer who has found a new
star, the explorer who leaps upon a shore
which his feet are the first to touch, and
even the poet himself when laurels are
thick upon him, does not feel the exultation which throbs in the boy who sees his
earliest song in print, and stands trembling
at the portals of the temple which enshrines
those who have enriched the world with
good books.   It is only a mirage, perhaps ;
but though it fades and leaves him far away
from that glorious company, for the moment it dazzles his sight.

A few bits of prose and verse in the
columns of a country paper, for which he

received no pay, were followed by " A New Year's Address," written for the carriers of the " Niagara Courier ; " and this was the first literary work which brought him money. The amount was one dollar and a half, not a large sum, to be sure, but it convinced him that literature was his proper vocation ; and he set out for New-York City to earn a living by his pen.

Even now, when publishers pay twenty times as much as they did then, an un-known lad coming to the city with such a purpose would have the hardest kind of a struggle. The chances are ten to one, that after a period of semi-starvation and repeated disappointments, he would have to give up, and seek his bread in some other employment. In Trowbridge's youth the circumstances were still harder, but his ambition was justified and fortified by a natural gift which was bound to find recog-nition. He had to climb the editorial stairs very often, and to go down them with a heavy heart, — a heart so heavy that if the rejected manuscript had been lead, it could not have made it heavier, — before success came to him. Once he had to drop the pen altogether, and to work at engraving gold pencil-cases in Jersey City, an employment which, if less congenial, was much more certain in its rewards than literature.

" I was more than once reduced to my last loaf," he says in a fragment of autobiography which he intrusted to me. " I lodged at that time in a house on Broadway, nearly opposite the Café des Mille Colonnes, where a band used to come out upon a balcony in the summer evenings and play tunes which to this day I can never hear without being instantly transported back to my garret and my crust. I do not remember, however, that I once lost hope in the darkest of these dark hours."

When looking about for employment in New York, he took some verses to Major Noah, the editor of " The Sunday Times," who treated him with great kindness, and counselled him to make literature his profession, but to write prose instead of poetry. Major Noah introduced him to some publishers, and to the editor of " The Dollar

Magazine," which was so called because it was sent to subscribers for a dollar a year, though it earned a still further claim to the title by paying writers one dollar a page for their contributions. One of the stories which "The Dollar Magazine" accepted was copied into a popular London magazine, and into many publications in the United States ; and Trowbridge thought that his fortune was made. But he found it impossible to live by writing for one dollar a page ; and fancying that he had taken a step higher by sending to " The Knickerbocker Magazine " an article which was speedily published in its pages, he learned from the polite editor, with deep disappointment, that that highly respectable periodical never paid any thing at all for contributions from new writers.

Fame, which had been hovering over the garret in an uncertain way for some time, at last knocked at the door, however ; and the farm - boy became the distinguished author.

Mr. Trowbridge now lives about five miles from Boston, in the pleasant suburb of Arlington, where he has a pleasant home on the banks of the historic Spy Pond. He takes high rank as a poet and as a novelist, but his chief distinction has been won in the field of juvenile literature.

September 5: 91

My dear Mr Rideing

The article will in no sense be a review
of Dana's Life. Dana's Life will merely
suggest the singular interest taken in the
Commercial marine by the people of the U.S.
and the peculiar influence exercised over
the British forecastle by the American
sea-writer — notably Dana & Melville.
Most of our nautical working choruses
come from you. There is much under
this head that is not known. The article will be push whenever printed — but
I dare not pledge myself to send it to
you at once. Sincerely Yours

W. Clark Russell

WILLIAM CLARK RUSSELL.

I OFTEN hear it said that boys are not as crazy to go to sea as they used to be; that the charm of a sailor's life has been dispelled; that steamers making regular voyages from port to port, like ferry-boats, do not allow the imagination to play as it did when a voyage could be made only in a sailing ship, and when there were no ocean cables to keep us informed of arrivals and departures all over the world.

Imagination, of course, must have always had a good deal to do with the fascination of the sea; for a sailor's life has been recognized as a hard one in every period, and under all flags. But in the days of buccaneers and pirates, and when ships set forth on voyages to countries of which little or nothing was known, it was easier to lose sight of the privations to be endured than it is now when every land has been explored, and the traffic of the high seas has no more romance in it than a railway.

If the boys who think of going to sea are fewer than they were, however, the interest in nautical stories has not abated. Capt. Marryat has lost none of his charm, and a new writer of sea-stories has come up, whose works are said to be more popular in America than those of any other English novelist.

This is William Clark Russell, the author of "The Wreck of the Grosvenor," "A Sailor's Sweetheart," "The Lady Maud," and several other books with which the readers of these lines are probably acquainted. I have no doubt that the reason his books are liked so much is that they are full of realities, and that he has been a sailor himself, and knows whereof he writes.

Although an Englishman, he was born at the Carlton House, Broadway, New York, on the 24th of February, 1844. His father was a composer and singer; and it was natural that the son of the author of that cheery song, "A Life on the Ocean Wave," should make the sea his theme

when the time came for him to use a pen.
He also inherited some of his literary tastes
from his mother, who in her youth was
intimately associated with Charles Lamb,
De Quincey, Wordsworth, and Coleridge,
her father having been a brother of Charles
Lloyd the poet. But it was not until he
had been through many adventures, and
had tried his hand at other things, that he
became an author.

Returning to Europe, his father went to
live at Boulogne, France, in a house named
Château Lettsom, after the celebrated Dr.
Lettsom, who had once occupied it; and
here Clark Russell's early years were passed.
He went to a private school in the town,
and he found among his fellow-scholars
three sons of Charles Dickens, — Frank,
Alfred, and Sydney. Frank became his
chum; they read the same stories, dreamed
the same dreams, and by and by, when
both were about eleven years of age, they
conspired to run away from school and
enter upon an expedition which was bound
to make their fortunes. The purpose of
the expedition was to shoot eider-ducks in

Norway, of which they had read in some
books of travel; and they calculated that
the wealth of "Monte Cristo" would be
exceeded by their profits from the sale
of the feathers. But Frank Dickens was
called home before their plans were ma-
tured; and his companion was doomed to
remain at school two years more, at the
end of which his parents decided that his
wish to go to sea should be gratified.

Those who have read "My Watch Below" and "The Voyage to the Cape" will
call to mind that in the former there is
a story, "The Middie's Yarn," and in the
latter a chapter called "It Acted Like a
Charm." Both of these fragments are
autobiographical, and if I wanted to deter
a boy from going to sea I would not fail to
place them in his hands.

A berth as a midshipman was found for
Clark Russell in one of Duncan Dunbar's
merchant ships, and the little fellow (only
thirteen and a half years old) was sent
down to the East India Docks in London
to join her. It was a day of dreams and
exultation for him, no doubt; he pictured

himself as another " Robinson Crusoe ; "
and he swelled with self-importance when,
after struggling along the crowded wharves
and dodging in and out among the piles
of merchandise, he passed the gangway,
and stood upon the deck of his ship (*his*
ship !) with the masts and spars and rig-
ging criss-crossing the sky high above
him.

When a boy wants to go to sea in America, he must get an appointment to the
Naval Academy at Annapolis, if he wishes
to enter the United-States service on a
higher grade than that of the common
sailor ; and if he is content with the mer-
chant-service, the only thing he can do is
to ship as a foremast hand, and subject himself to all the miseries of life in the forecastle. On many English ships, however,
it is the custom to take midshipmen ; and
in view of the fact that they are berthed
apart from the crew, they or their parents
are required to pay a good round sum to
the owners. This is what was done in the
case of Clark Russell ; but he found, as
many boys had done before and have done

since, that the amount paid as a " premium,"
as it is called, was money thrown away, and
that the lot of a midshipman in the mer-
chant-service is every bit as rough as that
of poor Jack Tar in the forecastle. He had
not been on board many hours before he
regretted the choice he had made, and the
life of an adventurous mariner seemed very
much less attractive than it had done in
the story-books.

The space allotted to the midshipmen
was " 'tween decks," a dark, narrow bit of
a room, with a table on stanchions running
down it ; and when Clark Russell stumbled
into it, those who were to be his mess-
mates were already there, skylarking, smok-
ing, and stowing their mattresses in their
bunks.

" Youngster," cried one of them, recog-
nizing him as soon as he entered, " why
don't you go down on all fours, and wag
your tail ? Don't you know you're a dog ?
You must be a dog, or you wouldn't go to
sea. The sea's only a fit life for dogs."

" Stop till he's slung aloft to scrape
down the mizzen-royal-mast in a gale of

wind," said another; "then he'll find out
why he's come to sea. — D'ye know where
the mizzen-royal-mast is kept stowed?
Go and ask the skipper to light you down
into the lazarette, where you'll find the
butcher's mate shelling pease. He has
charge of the mizzen-mast, and is the only
man allowed to serve out new dead-eyes
when the ship's figure-head goes adrift and
stops the fellow at the wheel from obeying
orders."

The boy could not understand this
"chaff," but it was more endurable than
the rough usage which followed.

The first night at sea, a storm arose ; and
as the green-hand lay deadly sick in his
bunk, he did not expect that he would have
to get up when all hands were called to
reef topsails. But, sick as he was, he was
dragged on to his feet, and sent aloft. It
was pitch dark, the rain driving along as if
it meant to blind a man, and the wind
blowing a gale ; but he knew it would not
do to skulk, and he staggered up the
companion-way, and began to haul on a
rope. Seeing him doing this, the third

mate roared out his name, and ordered
him to lay aft and jump aloft and help the
other midshipmen to reef the mizzen-
topsail.

The mizzen-topsail again! How hateful it sounded! "All three topsail
halyards were loose," he tells us in "The
Middie's Yarn," and "the canvas was
banging in the darkness like great guns
going off, all the crew, and idlers as well,
singing out at the ropes, and the second
mate in the waist and the chief mate aft
shouting at the top of their voices."

He got into the lee shrouds, and climbed
up until he came to the mizzen-top; but
once there he was too dizzy and too weak
to go higher. He sat down dreadfully
sick, and wished himself dead. His cap
was blown off his head, his boots were full
of water, and, as he had no oilskins on, he
was soaked to the skin by the rain and the
spray. Here the sailors found him, and
one of them, taking pity on him, shoved
him through the "lubber's hole," and
helped him down on deck again.

This was only the beginning; and when

he came to have as little fear of going
aloft as the best of them, he still had to
put up with poor and insufficient food, and
with all kinds of drudgery.

"I've scraped and greased down masts,"
he says, "painted the ship's side, tarred
down, cleaned the brass-work, painted the
quarter-boats; and I only wonder that
the skipper didn't put us to washing
up the cuddy-dishes and cleaning the
knives."

Taking his own word for it that "The
Middie's Yarn" is autobiographical, we
find another passage in that sketch which
shows us how much he endured on his
first voyage : —

"I was in the chief mate's watch, — the
port watch, it's called. Well, suppose we
have the middle watch in ; at four o'clock
we're turned out and come on deck. It's
still dark, and there's nothing to be done
if the wind's steady and the ship is holding
her course. But soon after the sun rises
the pumps are rigged, and the watch turns
to and washes the decks down. If it's
fine warm weather, I pull off my boots; if

not, I keep them on — sea-boots, of course. The midshipmen have to scrub the poop down; they lay hold of the brushes, and the third mate swills the water along. That was our way; but, of course, customs are different in different ships. We scrub under the hencoops, scrub the gratings abaft the wheel, clean the paint-work, and when that housemaid's job is over we swab and coil down and make the poop fit for the passengers to enjoy themselves upon. By the time all this is done, the brass-work cleaned, and so forth, it's past seven bells, and we go below to breakfast. I've already described our cabin, but you could never understand it without seeing a drawing of it. I once killed twenty-eight cockroaches in my bunk in twelve minutes. It wasn't only that our cabin was dark, and lumbered up with table and bunks, and our 'stores' stowed away in a corner alongside a dresser full of plates and dishes: we had a heap of emigrants in the 'tween decks; and what with the womens quabbling, and the children squalling, and the men growling, the row al!

day long was like an Irish riot. I say
nothing of the different smells of the food
and the washing-tubs. Well, we'd go below to breakfast; but what was there to
eat? Biscuit, with a bit of yesterday's
pork or beef, — but seldom that, for, bad
as the food was, we youngsters were never
so well supplied with salt meat but that
we weren't always ready to eat each other's
allowance, — and some black liquor called
tea, with a mass of short yellow sticks floating atop of it. When I used to look at
that food, how my conscience would prick
me for having turned up my nose at the
dinners on my father's table, saying, as I
used to, to my mother, 'Mutton again —
it's always mutton!' Or, 'Apple-tart!
Why don't you give us plum-pudding for
a change?' I'd have put up with mutton
and apple-tart every day at sea, for months
at a stretch, could I've got 'em. After
breakfast the starboard watch would go on
deck, and we of the port watch would turn
in. At a quarter before twelve we'd rouse
out to get dinner. This consisted of pork
or beef. If it was pork day, we'd have

some lukewarm, greasy water with a few dozen of yellow shot knocking about in it, called pea-soup, served out to us; if beef day, we'd get a calker of duff, looking to the eye like old yellow soap, and tasting — well, and tasting like duff; and more than that I can't say. Sometimes we'd have a few of our own preserved spuds — spuds means potatoes — cooked; but I could never endure the smell, much less the taste, of those things. Then we'd go on deck, where we'd be set to work at once on different jobs."

One voyage of this kind would cure any boy who had only a fancy for the sea, and send him home penitent; but Clark Russell had a deep love of blue water, and though he found that a sailor's life was not just what he had pictured it to be, there were charms in it that induced him to remain in the service of Duncan Dunbar. From midshipman he rose to be mate; and he made voyages to Australia, Madras, Calcutta, Hong Kong, and other places. On one occasion he lay for ten months in the Gulf of Pe-Chee-Lee, his ship being a transport carrying troops from Calcutta.

While he was still a very young man, however, he gave up the sea as a calling; and after two months spent in a stock-broker's office, he took up the pen, and entered on a literary career. Did he find this much easier than the sea? Not in the beginning. He sent a novel to an eminent firm of publishers; and after eight months of weary waiting, his manuscript was returned to him, " in a basket, like a leg of mutton," as he says. Other attempts were more successful, but the novel by which he afterward made his mark was rejected by at least one publisher before it was accepted. This was " The Wreck of the Grosvenor." Since that he has gone on writing sea stories, and it is his own experiences that give them life and interest.

EDWARD EGGLESTON.

ONE of the chief uses of biography is in the power it has to cheer up those whose lives are beset with difficulties, and to awaken aspiration where hope has scarcely dared to sit. Many a boy has learned from the printed page the lesson that Bow bells rang out to Dick Whittington, and has found his courage renewed for fresh endeavor by the example set forth in the narrative of some life in which a greater adversity than his own has been doggedly resisted and overcome. Turning over the leaves of the book, he has seen the black letters of despair vanish, and all earthly attainments made possible to the youth who has patience and industry.

Such a lesson as this, not a new one, to be sure, is brought home to us once more when we look at the boyhood of Edward Eggleston, whose stories, among which are

<u>From the Hoosier Schoolboy.</u>

So then, you see, this world of ours is just like the House that Jack Built; one thing is tied to another, and another to that, and that to this, and this to something, and something to something else, and so on to the very end of all things.

Edward Eggleston

"The Hoosier Schoolmaster," "The Mystery of Metropolisville," and "The End of the World," have placed him among the most successful and most original writers of fiction in America, while he has added to the distinction thus acquired by his work as an editor, an historian, and a poet.

He was born on the 10th of December, 1837, at Vevay, Indiana, — a country boy who had to contend not only with the disadvantages which loom up before every country boy who wants to lead an intellectual life, but also with frequent illnesses which came and paralyzed the hand when the lamp of ambition burned the brightest, and showed Fame in her most alluring garb.

A country boy is at a certain disadvantage in the matter of education now, but his opportunities are incalculably greater than what they were in the days of Edward Eggleston's boyhood. Then the rule of three was the objective point of all study, and it was thought that he who had ciphered through that had well-nigh exhausted human knowledge. The schoolmaster himself was often unable to spell the simplest words.

"The teaching was absurd," Mr. Eggleston says in one of his sketches. "I was made to go through Webster's spelling-book five times before I was thought fit to begin to read, and my mother, twenty years earlier, spelled it through nine times before she was allowed to begin Lindley Murray's 'English Reader.' As I recall the old-time school, I cannot but think that if its discipline was somewhat more brutal than the school discipline of to-day, its course of study was far less so. To a nervous child the old discipline was, indeed, very terrible. The long birch switches hanging on hooks against the wall haunted me night and day from the time I entered one of the old schools. And whenever there came an outburst between master and pupils, the thoughtless child often got the beating that should have fallen upon the malicious mis-chief-makers. As the master was always quick to fly into a passion, the fun-loving boys were always happy to stir him up. It was an exciting sport, like bull-baiting, or like poking sticks through a fence at a cross dog. Sometimes the ferocious master showed an ability on his own part to get some fun out of the conflict, as when on one occasion in a school in Ohio the boys were forbidden to attend a circus. Five or six of them went in spite of the prohibition. The next morning the schoolmaster called them out on the floor, and addressed them : —

"'So you went to the circus, did you?'

"'Yes, sir.'

"'Well, the others did not get a chance to see the circus. I want you boys to show them what it looked like, and how the horses galloped around the ring. You will join your hands in a circle about the stove. Now start!'

"With that he began whipping them as they trotted around and around the stove."

But, few as the opportunities were, there never was a time in Indiana when a good school was not accounted a thing of the greatest value, and Mr. Eggleston tells a story of a raw-boned boy who knocked at the schoolmaster's door early one winter's morning to ask how he should do a " sum " which puzzled him. He had ridden a farm-horse many miles for this purpose, and had to be back home in time to begin his day's work as usual. The kind-hearted school-master, chafing his hands to keep them warm, sat down by the boy, and taught him how to do the " sum." Then the poor little fellow straightened himself up, and, thrusting his hand into his trousers pocket, pulled out a quarter of a dollar, explaining with a blush that it was all he could pay, for it was all he had. Of course the master made him put it back, and told him to come whenever he wanted any help.

The father of Edward Eggleston was a Virginian, a graduate of William and Mary College, who went to Indiana in early man-hood, and achieved a place among the foremost men at the bar in the West. He died when he was a little more than thirty years of age, but he had already spent no little time in moulding the character of Ed-ward, who was his oldest child. One day he said to him, —

" I'll tell you what my father told me, and

his father told him, — never tell a lie, and knock down any man that says you do."

The Egglestons were Southerners, and had always lived up to this family precept; but Edward omitted the knocking down part. On another occasion, when his father was a candidate for Congress, he said to the son, —

" I'm not going to live very long. Never do you have any thing to do with politics. In politics a man is as much disgusted with the rascality of his friends as of his enemies."

It was not an eventful boyhood, this of Edward Eggleston. Part of it was spent in farm labor, and part in a country store. All his school days did not cover more than two years, and he may claim to be self-educated. Until he was ten years old he had the reputation of being dull despite his shrewdness, but after that he never had a schoolmate who could acquire knowledge more rapidly. He got more out of his habit of reading than out of his attendance at school, and he learned several languages by solitary study.

" Of the books that impressed me deeply when I was a boy," he says in a letter to the author of this sketch, " I remember particularly Franklin's autobiography, certain essays of Bishop Thomson, Young's ' Night-Thoughts,' and Pope's poetry, especially the ' Essay on Man.' When I was a little less than sixteen I was strongly impressed by Priestley's ' Exposition of the Hartleian System of Mental Philosophy,' and by Locke on the ' Conduct of the Human Understanding.' At sixteen I read with keen relish, but without entire agreement, certain of Lord Jeffrey's essays. I read few novels, for I was brought up a Methodist. I remember the delight I had at seventeen in Milton's ' Paradise Lost,' Irving's ' Sketch Book,' and Virgil's Eclogues, which last I read in the original alone. I was throughout my childhood and youth strongly influenced by Methodist literature, of which I read much, for my life was double. I was almost an enthusiast on one side, and a lad with a strong bent toward literature and learning on the other."

Ambitious as he was to be a scholar, there were weeks and months when he could not study, owing to illness, and the enforced idleness was a sore trial to him. Every road seemed barred to him by his ill health and uncertain tenure of life. There were times, however, when he was strong enough to take long walks with his brother, George Cary Eggleston, who has also become a notable author. They spent days together tramping over the hills and revelling in the beauties of the landscape spread out before them from the summits. They followed a plan of Edward's devising to economize strength, and secure the best results of exertion. He had observed that long rests stiffen the muscles, and he there fore determined that they should walk steadily for ten minutes, and then rest for three. This they did frequently for an entire day, from sunrise to sunset, without apparent hurt even to him; and to harden themselves still more, as they thought, they gave up their beds, and slept on the floor of their room. Edward made their walks still more interesting by his knowledge of geol-

ogy, and gave the history of trilobites
which George knocked out of perilous
places in the face of the cliffs.   Naturally
Edward was too great an invalid for many
of the sports of his playfellows.   He was
only a middling ball player, but he was a
first-rate hand at king's base, which requires the fleetness of foot which he possessed in a remarkable degree, and in
" bull-pen " — an old Middle State game, —
he was the best dodger of them all.

"In all intellectual ways," says one of
his old schoolfellows, " he was the recognized captain of every school he ever attended.   Curiously enough he maintained
another sort of ascendency less easily accounted for.   We were a robust set of fellows, rough in sport and energetic in all
physical ways, and usually we had pity
rather than sympathy or respect for physical weakness ; but Edward always commanded the school on the playground as
well as elsewhere.   His word was as nearly
law with us as any thing could be among a
rather lawless set of youngsters.   He was
never thought of as a weakling at all ; he

asked no odds of anybody on account of
his illness, and he took all his knocks as
manfully as the most robust of us. But
the peculiar regard in which he was held
by his companions, and the undisputed
command he exercised upon occasions,
were due in a large part to two facts : first,
that we all recognized him as our superior
in knowledge and ability; and, secondly,
that we knew him to be just in all his judg-
ments and absolutely without fear or favor."

When he was about seventeen years old,
he went in quest of health among his father's relatives in Virginia, and for five
months he attended a boarding-school in
Amelia County. This was the last schooling he ever had. His health continued
poor, and in 1856, two years later, he went
to Minnesota, where he became a jack-of-
all-trades. He made himself useful on a
farm, he joined the chain-gang of a sur-
veying party, and he opened a photograph-
gallery.

Then he returned to his native State,
and, having always had a deep religious
feeling, he started out as a circuit preacher,

travelling from town to town with the Gospel in his saddle-bags. From hut to hut, we ought to say, rather than from town to town, for the path of the circuit preacher lay through the wilderness to places in which there were no regular churches.

All this time, however, he was gathering materials for the stories that were afterward to make him famous. As many others have done, he made his entrance into the profession of literature through journalism, which is a sort of half-sister to it; and he was successively connected with "The Little Corporal" (then an excellent magazine for young people), "The Independent" and "Hearth and Home," a once popular weekly. It was while he was editor of the latter that he wrote "The Hoosier Schoolmaster," which a distinguished critic has said is as faithful a picture of life in Southern Indiana forty years ago as Sir Walter Scott's "Ivanhoe" is of life in England after the Norman conquest. Its success was extraordinary from the appearance of the first instalment; and, when it afterward came out in book form, it rivalled in popularity " Uncle Tom's Cabin " and " Little Women." Even now, after fifteen years, it sells better than most new works ; and the reason is, that it is true to life. It has been followed by half a dozen other stories, among which are " Roxy " and " The Hoosier Schoolboy." We are probably not violating a confidence in repeating what the author has said to us : " I have drawn my native village — Vevay, Indiana — in ' Roxy ' and in ' The Hoosier Schoolboy ; ' and my stories are full of the reflections of my childhood, but of undiluted autobiography there is little."

As the dusk was setting in on a beautiful autumnal day about thirty-seven years ago, a man and a boy were driving a cow along a country road in Ohio. They had come a long distance, and were weary ; but though the boy limped, the conversation did not flag as they trudged along ; and you might have seen that while they talked with such animation, they were alive to the gold and crimson of the autumn woods, which seemed to have borrowed their flashes of color from the sunset sky.

They were evidently not farmers ; both had the appearance of living a city life, but had they been observed, the things they were saying, and not their looks, would have attracted attention ; for they were talking of Cervantes and Shakspeare.

The cow needed much urging, and it was late at night when they reached some

Thanksgiving

I.

Lord, for the erring thought
Not into evil wrought;
Lord, for the wicked will
Betrayed and baffled still;
For the heart from itself kept,
Our thanksgiving accept.

II.

For ignorant hopes that were
Broken to our blind prayer;
For pain, death, sorrow, sent
Unto our chastisement;
For all loss of seeming good
Quicken our gratitude.

W. D. Howells.

white-limbed sycamores beside the tail-race
of a grist-mill on the Little Miami River,
on the other side of which was the small
log cabin in which they lived. A question
then arose as to how they should get the
cow across. They did not know the depth
of the water, but they knew it to be cold,
and they did not care to swim it. The
elder wanted the boy to run up under the
sycamores to the saw-mill, cross the head-
race there, and come back to receive the
cow on the other side of the tail-race. But
with all his literature, the boy was young
enough to be superstitious, and afraid of
the dark ; and though the elder urged him
to go, he would not force him. They could
see the lights in the cabin twinkling cheerfully, and they shouted to those within, but
no one heard them. They called and
called in vain, and were answered only by
the cold rush of the tail-race, the rustle of
sycamore leaves, and the homesick lowing
of the cow.

They determined to drive her across
from the shore, and then to run up to the
saw-mill and down the other bank, so as to

catch her as she reached it. When they came there, she was not to be found, however; she had instantly turned again, and during the night she made her way back to the town from which they had brought her.

The log cabin was a small one, with a cornfield of eighty acres behind it, and it was nearly a quarter of a century old. The boy who entered it after this adventure was William Dean Howells, and the man was his father, who had recently brought his family from Dayton to take charge of the saw-mill and grist-mill on the river. The incident illustrates, with what follows, the simplicity of the early life of one who has since become one of the foremost American novelists.

Mr. Howells was born March 1, 1837, at Martin's Ferry, Ohio, opposite Wheeling, West Virginia. His father was of Welsh descent, his mother of German stock, and both were superior by education and tastes to the moderate circumstances in which they found themselves when this boy, who was one of eight children, came into the world. When he was only three years old, they left Martin's Ferry to live in Hamilton, Ohio, and there the father bought and edited the " Intelligencer," a weekly newspaper, and his son was scarcely out of his cradle before he learned to set type. He had little regular schooling, but he was a great reader, and had a natural gift for composition. He does not remember how young he was when he mastered the mysteries of the printer's trade, but it·was certainly long before he was twelve ; at that age he remembers having helped in his father's office to set in type President Zachary Taylor's inaugural message.

There were leisure moments between the working hours, and he occupied these in printing compositions of his own. However precocious they may be, few young authors see their work immortalized by the dignity and permanence of type before they reach their teens ; but when this lad was only eleven, he set up and printed an ambitious work of his own. A thoroughbred is not less fearless of ditch and hedge than the budding author is of the magnitude of his theme.   A veteran will stoop to write about rag-pickers or Punch and Judy, and go afoot in search of a commonplace subject ; but the beginner plunges his spurs into the flanks of Pegasus, and sends the winged horse galloping along the edge of the dizziest precipices of Olympus.   Mr. Howells is called a "realist" now.   He writes about men and women as they are, and will have neither villains of deep dye nor paragons of virtue in his stories : for he believes that good and evil are mixed in all of us.   But he was of a different mind when he wore a white apron, and stood before the printer's case, with its alphabetical compartments full of little metal letters.   He boldly launched out then, not in any cockle-shell of rhyme, but in a five-act blank-verse tragedy ; and it should be needless to say that the subject was the death of a Roman emperor.   Such ventures carry too much sail for their ballast; and, like other lightly laden ships, this has not been heard from since.

The literary ambition was fixed in him while he was very young, and it was stimulated by the scholarly tastes of his father and by his own appetite for reading. In a desultory way he went first to a public and then to a private school. His favorite study was history, and the study he cared least for, and for which he had the least aptitude, was arithmetic. He liked to read aloud, and could do it well. Probably he lost less through the infrequency and irregularity of his attendance than many others would have done, for he was one of the exceptional boys who do more for their education by observation and by reading, than schoolmasters are able to do for them.

His favorite book at this period of his life was Goldsmith's History of Greece, and side by side with it in his estimation were "Don Quixote" and the inexhaustible delights of the "Arabian Nights." The first novel he read was "The Trippings of Tom Pepper; or, the Effects of Romancing," and the moral it was intended to inculcate struck him so sharply that he entered into a solemn pledge with his brother to avoid prevarication under every circumstance. His admiration for "Don

Quixote" was so great that the author of
it became his hero, and instead of content-
ing himself with the romance of the "mad
knight" and Sancho Panza, as most readers do, he read besides the other works of
the great Spanish author Cervantes, whom
he still reckons as a peer of Shakspeare.
He was a rather delicate boy, and though
he was fond of outdoor sports and games,
he was not expert in any one of them.

In 1849 his father sold the "Intelligencer," and moved his family to Dayton,
where he purchased another paper, called
the "Transcript," which he changed from
a semi-weekly to a daily.   This movement
was not a success, and at the end of two
years the failure of it was confessed.   All·
the editor's sons, of whom there were four,
could set type, and all of them had helped
in producing the paper.   After working in
the composing-room until eleven at night,
the boy we are writing about was often
obliged to get up at four to carry the
paper and deliver it to subscribers.   But
the boys took their misfortunes cheerfully,
and when the last issue was printed, they

all went down to the Miami and had a good swim.

It was then that they took possession of the log cabin, and the year they spent there has been beautifully described by Mr. Howells himself. They did not regret this change from town to country. The father's passionate fondness for nature had been nourished by the English poets, and he had taught his children all that he felt for the woods and fields and open skies. They glazed the narrow windows, relaid the rotten floor, patched the roof, and papered the walls.

"Perhaps it was my father's love of literature which inspired him to choose newspapers for this purpose," says Mr. Howells; "at any rate he did so, and the effect, as I remember it, was not without its decorative qualities. He had used a barrel of papers bought at the nearest post-office, where they had been refused by the persons to whom they had been experimentally sent by the publisher; and the whole first page was taken up by a story which broke off in the middle of a sentence at the foot of the last column, and tantalized us forever with fruitless conjectures as to the fate of the hero and heroine."

It took some days to make the repairs ; but when they were completed, the boys laid their mattresses on the sweet, new oak-plank of the floor, and slept hard — in every sense. One night they awoke, and saw their father sitting upright in his bed.

"What are you doing?" they asked.

" Oh, resting!" he answered, jokingly referring to the hardness of his bed.

Their life was full of privations, but it was sweetened by their love of nature and their unfailing good-humor. The boys slept in the loft. "The rude floor rattled and wavered loosely under our tread, and the window in the gable stood open or shut at its own will. There were cracks in the shingle through which we could see the stars, and which, when the first snow came, let the flakes sift in upon the floor. I should not like to step out of bed into a snow-wreath in the morning, now ; but then I was glad to do it, and so far from thinking that or any thing in our life a hardship, I counted it all joy.

"Our barrels of paper-covered books were stowed away in the loft, and, over-hauling them one day, I found a paper copy of the poems of a certain Henry Wadsworth Longfellow, then wholly un-known to me; and while the old grist-mill, whistling and wheezing to itself, made a vague music in my ears, my soul was filled with this strange, new sweetness. I read 'The Spanish Student' there, and 'Coplas de Manrique,' and the solemn and ever-beautiful 'Voices of the Night.' There were other books in those barrels which I must have read also, but I remember only those that spirited me again to Spain, where I had already been with Irving, and led me to attack seriously the old Spanish grammar, which had been knocking about our house ever since my father bought it from a soldier of the Mexican war. But neither those nor any other books made me discontented with the small-boy's world around me. They made it a little more populous with visionary shapes, but that was well, and there was room for them all. It was not darkened with cares, and the duties in it were not many."

At the end of a year the foreman of a printing office in Xenia came to the log cabin, and asked the boy to take the place of a delinquent hand, as he was known to be a good compositor, swift and clean and steady. He tried the job, and gave satisfaction; but time did not cure the homesickness he felt on leaving the simple little cabin in the woods, and he was obliged to return; few as its comforts were, he was held to it by a bond of affection which no offer of worldly prosperity could induce him to break. As long as the family remained there, he staid with them; and when at last they again went to live in the town, he took a place as compositor on the "Ohio State Journal," at a salary of four dollars a week.

For several years after this, his literary ambitions were subordinated to the necessities of mechanical labor as a printer and reporter, but all the time he was equipping himself for a higher and better kind of

work ; he added French and Italian to his
knowledge of languages, and made the
great authors of the world his companions.
Then one morning he gathered courage
to knock at the door of " The Atlantic
Monthly" with a bundle of verses in his
hand, and they were so good that the
editor accepted and printed them.

His advance was rapid after that, and
in time he became the editor of the
" Atlantic," a position which he held for
nine years. Meanwhile, he was doing original work of his own, and he has earned
distinction as a poet, as a writer of plays,
and, above all, as a novelist.

Quite recently he went back to the place
where the old log cabin had stood, but it
was there no more. Thirty years had
passed, and all that had happened since
seemed so much like a dream, that, when
he spoke of his boyhood to a little fellow
who followed him, he himself could scarcely believe that what he told was true, and
he says that he had a sense of imposing
upon his listener.

IT must be quite twenty years ago that I read a story called " A Perfect Treasure," as it came out week after week in a certain English magazine. The leading character was a youth with literary aspirations, and it was like reading one's own autobiography to follow his adventures in search of a publisher ; the application of his experiences as possibilities to one's self was much more fascinating than the plot.

If my memory is not at fault, a carriage runs away in the story, and the hero stops the horses, an incident which is always turning up, like the proverbial bad sixpence ; but in this case the occupant of the carriage does not prove to be a beautiful heiress, nor does she instantly fall in love with her deliverer, as she might be expected to do. It is not a young and lovely person at all, but an old lady whom the hero recognizes as a famous authoress liv-

My dear Riding

Remember to
you kindly sketch.
Send me the book
when it appears,
please.
I enclose a copy
of my portrait as
desired.
Yours &c
James Payn

ing in the neighborhood; and instead of marrying him and sharing a fortune with him, she only becomes his friend, and helps him to get a start in literature.

Something in the character made me think at the time that it was drawn from life, though the runaway was, of course, an invention; and many years afterward when I met James Payn, the author of the story, he admitted to me that the original was Mary Russell Mitford, who was actually his own literary godmother.

She had been a friend of his father's, and lived at Swallowfield, not far from his own home at Maidenhead, on the Thames; and she was a constant friend to the son, guiding him with advice and criticism, and opening doors for him which less fortunate beginners find closed and barred. A literary godmother is a useful relation, and though she cannot make an author out of a boy who has no gift for literature, her experience and connections enable her to clear the way for one who has ability, and only needs opportunity. Such a boy was James Payn.

She at first tried to dissuade him from making literature a profession, by pointing out its inevitable trials; and, failing in this, she used her influence to advance him in the great world of literature which he was bound to explore. How sound her advice was, he proved by experience, and though he has vindicated the wisdom of his own course, he has re-echoed in his maturity her voice of warning for the benefit of the present generation : —

"There is no pursuit so doubtful, so full of risks, so subject to despondency and disappointments, so open to despair itself," he says, in one of his books. " Oh, my young friend, with 'a turn for literature,' think twice and thrice before committing yourself to it, or you may bitterly regret to find yourself where that 'turn' may take you! The literary calling is an exceptional one, and even at the best you will have trials and troubles of which you dream not, and to which no other calling is exposed."

This is distinctly of a piece with the advice Miss Mitford gave him; but as her admonition did not hold him back, his, I am afraid, will not restrain the ambitious youth who sees more glory in the pen than in the sword or the sceptre.

The letters she wrote to him were recently in my possession, — a bundle of them, tattered and stained, after the hoarding of forty years or more, and written in a small, crabbed, angular hand, which, after filling all sides of the paper with the closest lines, had economized still further by running edgewise along the margin; even the flaps of the envelopes had been utilized for microscopic postscripts. I wish every boy who is thinking of literature as a profession might read them.

"Be careful as to style," she wrote, in one of them; "give as much character as you can, and as much *truth*, that being the foundation of all merit in literature and art." This was after her attempt to dissuade him from entering on a literary career had failed, and previous to it she had endeavored to induce him to devote himself to a business life, and make literature the recreation of his leisure. As an

example of what could be done in this direction she pointed out a merchant, whom
we may call Mr. A. "If I had fifty sons
they should all be in trade," she declared,
in another of the letters. "It is the most
independent career, the most useful, the
most powerful for good, as the press is the
most powerful for evil. I wish you knew
Mr. A., — his frankness, his cordiality, his
cheerfulness, his universal information, his
knack of bringing friends together, his perfect high-breeding. If you knew Mr. A.
you would see at once that the calling
which such a man has followed can have
nothing in it that is not honorable. He
and James T. Fields, the American book-
seller (for these great publishers keep a
store), are by far the most princely persons
in heart and manner whom I have ever
known, and each of them has made his
own fortune — the one at five-and-thirty,
certainly not more — the other, perhaps,
ten years older, — both with hair as glossy
and curly as your own, and not a single
silver thread among the curls."

Nothing but literature would satisfy his

soul, however; he would not stoop to a desk and a ledger, through Mr. A. was willing to give him employment which would have allowed him from five o'clock to ten for his poetic studies, " more by four hours, on an average, than I ever had," that gentleman wrote. But the boy's resolve was inflexible, and authorship in an attic, even with only a crust to eat, seemed better than commerce and affluence.

This was when he was about seventeen or eighteen years old; and it will be interesting now to look back to his earlier years. His family held an excellent social position, and his education was amply provided for. First he was sent to a preparatory school; then to Eton; next to the Military Academy at Woolwich; and finally to Trinity College, Cambridge, from which he was graduated in 1854. He was not a studious boy in the sense of one who rapidly memorizes lessons, and shines at examinations; he had the usual antipathy of persons with a literary bent for mathematics and formulas of all kinds: but he was a diligent reader, and picked up knowledge in the unseen and unconscious ways which are unintelligible and impracticable to closer and more systematic scholars.

He was, no doubt, thought a queer boy by his schoolfellows, but he had one gift that made him popular, as it has done since in a much larger circle. He was a born story-teller, and could weave the most wonderful stories out of his own head. Many a night he was compelled to sit up in bed romancing until one after another the older boys fell asleep.

His school life was unhappy, both at the preparatory school and at Eton. Fagging, or hazing, prevailed at the latter school, and flogging too. The head master was a dandified gentleman, who held the birch with jewelled fingers.

" Please, sir, it's my first fault," the culprit would sometimes plead.

" I think I remember your name before," the pedagogue would reply to this.

" It was my brother, sir."

" Very well, I'll look at my book ; " and the boy would shuffle away reprieved.

One boy, seventeen years of age, who

was leaving Eton to enter the army, was
flogged a few days before his departure.
It was a custom then (it may be still) for
the boys to present the master with a ten-
pound note when they left, dropping it
delicately into a jar where he could find
it after they had gone. But smarting from
his punishment the departing scholar only
pretended to drop his ten-pound note into
the jar, and chuckled as he pictured to
himself the master's fruitless hunt after
that precious bit of tissue paper. " I can't
flog him for flogging me unjustly," he reflected, " but, dash it, I can *fine* him."

The boys in the higher classes were fond
of snubbing and patronizing those of the
lower classes. " Lower Boy, what might
be your name?" a diminutive fellow, with
a white choker, inquired in a drawling voice
of Payn one day.

" Well, it *might* be Beelzebub, but it
isn't," Payn replied; whereupon the " fifth-
form " boy attempted to thrash him. " It
was the only proper punishment for
'cheek,' no doubt, but I thought it hard
that a repartee should be so ill-received,"

the victim has since said in describing this incident.

Unless a boy had a taste for the classics, Eton in those days did little for him, except in establishing certain moral attributes; and at the end of a year or so Payn, who cared more for Shakspeare than for all the Greeks, went away from the gray old academic buildings with little added to his stock of knowledge. Resolute as he was in his choice of a profession, his relatives still persisted in other plans for him, and they now procured a nomination for him to the Military Academy at Woolwich, which, except that it educates boys for the British army, is identical in its purpose with the academy at West Point.

To prepare him for Woolwich, he was sent to another preparatory establishment, and the system of " cramming" practised here was more hateful to him than anything at his first school or at Eton. He had long and tedious lessons to learn of which he never knew the meaning, and he recited them as mechanically as a phonograph. The purpose of the school was not to instruct the mind and develop the reason, but to make the pupil *seem* to be familiar with studies of which he was ignorant. The master was confident that Payn could pass the ordinary examination, but was afraid he could not stand the physical test, as he was near-sighted.

"The examiners at Woolwich," said the master, "will tell you to look out of the window and describe the colors of the horses on the common. Mind you say 'bay' or 'gray' very rapidly, for all horses are either bay or gray, and if you make a mistake they will not notice it." This illustrates the methods which were followed in all the studies.

The work was so hard and so continuous, that little time was left for reading; but while he was here, Payn had the delight of seeing his compositions published for the first time, though they were not yet printed. He had one schoolfellow named Raymond who could draw, another named Jones who could write like print, and a third named Barker who had a taste for finance. Together they started a weekly

paper full of stories and poems, for circulation among their companions. Payn provided the literary part, which Raymond
illustrated, and Jones made as many copies
as were needed. The circulation of the
paper was left to Barker, who fixed the
price at sixpence a copy. Their school-
fellows did not appreciate the venture, but
Barker was the treasurer of the school, and
held in trust for the scholars a certain
fund out of which he had to give them two
shillings weekly for pocket-money. Seeing that they would not buy the paper will-
ingly, he calmly deducted sixpence from
each allowance, and gave a copy of the
paper to make up for it. "The 'masses'
never know what is good for them," Mr.
Payn says, in referring to this, "and our
schoolfellows were no exception to the
rule ; they called Barker a Jew, and, so to
speak, 'murmured against Moses.' He
was tall and strong, and fought at least
half a dozen pitched battles for the mainte-
nance of his object ; I think he persuaded
himself, like Charles I., that he was really
in the right, and set down their opposition

to mere 'impatience of taxation,' but in the end they were one too many for him, and, indeed, much more than one. He fell fighting, no doubt, in the sacred cause of literature, but also for his own sixpences, for we — the workers — never saw one penny of them."

Payn succeeded in passing the examination at Woolwich, but he distinguished himself there by his humorous escapades rather than by his scholarship, and before he was seventeen he had to resign on account of illness. His friends then decided that he should enter the Church, and he was sent to a private tutor's to be prepared for the university.

He was more content now, and for the first and only time in his life found pleasure in out-door exercise. "I had some companions of my own age who taught me the use of the leaping-pole. We scoured the country with fourteen-foot poles in our hands, and rarely found brook or lane too broad for us. Many a time, like Commodore Trunion, have I astonished a wagoner by flying from steep bank to bank, over the heads of himself and his horses."

But the pen lost none of its attractions, and verse and prose poured from it. He went through all the agonies of the rejected contributor; time and again he dropped his poems and essays into the post-office, only to receive them back in a month or so with an intimation that they would not do, and the dream of fame faded away in the wintry morning of despair. The sun began to shine by and by, and never did it seem so splendid as the day when it revealed one of his poems printed in a periodical called "Leigh Hunt's Journal." Soon after this he wrote an article on cadet life at Woolwich, which was accepted by "Household Words," the paper edited by Charles Dickens. He thought that his fortune was made now, but there were many disappointments and many set-backs still in store for him. Fame is a coquettish maiden to woo, and pouts as easily as she smiles. The boy with his first article in print thinks he has won her, but, though she stands by his side for a moment, she

quickly runs away, and beckons to him
from a milestone farther along the road.
Payn had to pass many such milestones
before he came up with her. Many things
he wrote were published, but there was no
certain acceptance for his work, and much
of it came back. He published two little
books of poems, which were civilly treated
by the critics; he made the acquaintance
of Miss Mitford, who introduced him to
Harriet Martineau, and also through the
kindness of Miss Mitford he was introduced to De Quincey, the famous essayist
and opium-eater. At luncheon with De
Quincey, he was asked what wine he would
take, and he was about to pour out a glass
from the decanter that stood next to him,
when De Quincey's daughter whispered,
" You must not take that; it is not port
wine as you seem to think." It was, in
fact, laudanum, the drug to which her
father was the most pitiable slave, and he
presently helped himself to it as if it had
been wine.

A second time Fame seemed to have
taken the young author by the hand. The

publishers of a periodical placarded a story
which they had bought of him, over all the
walls of Cambridge, where he was an un-
dergraduate ; but he was again mistaken,
though, as he says, he was not the first to
confuse a placard on the wall with genuine
reputation. He had twenty-six articles rejected in one year, and it was fortunate that
he was not wholly dependent on his pen
for a living. He took his degree at the
University, and quickly added to his academic honors those which come by mar-
riage. His earnings for the first year of his
married life were thirty-two pounds fifteen
shillings, or about one hundred and sixty-
three dollars and seventy-five cents. The
tide was turning, however, and the next
year his income was quadrupled.

Mr. Payn is now the editor of the " Corn-
hill Magazine," and about a hundred volumes stand to his credit on the shelves of
the library of the British Museum. What
reader of English fiction is unfamiliar with
his stories, in which humor, and wit, and
great dramatic power are united ? He has
gone on improving in his art ever since

he sat up in bed inventing stories for his
schoolfellows, like a little Scheherezade,
and he is now a type of the prosperous
literary man; but he is modest, and it
seems to him, no doubt, that he has not yet
overtaken Fame, who is still beckoning
him another league ahead.

JOHN GREENLEAF WHITTIER.

THE life of Whittier may be read in his poems, and by putting a note here and a date there, a full autobiography might be compiled from them. His boyhood and youth are depicted in them with such detail that little need be added to make the story complete; and that little, reverently done as it may be, must seem poor in comparison with the poetic beauty of his own revelations.

What more can we do to show his early home than to quote from his own beautiful poem "Snow-Bound"? There the house is pictured for us, inside and out, with all its furnishings; and those who gathered around its hearth, inmates and visitors, are set before us so clearly that, long after the book has been put away, they remain as distinct in the memory as portraits that are visible day after day on the walls of our

The autumn haze lay soft and still
On wood and meadow and upland farms,
On the brow of Snow Hill the great windmill
Slowly and lazily swung its arms.
Broadly before them the turquoise bay
With its capes and islands stretched away,
And over meadows and dusk of pines
Blue hills lifted their faint outlines.
From the "King's Missive"

John G. Whittier

Oak Knoll
4/13 1888.

homes. He reproduces in his verse the landscapes he saw, the legends of witches and Indians he listened to, the school-fellows he played with, the voices of the woods and fields, and the round of toil and pleasure in a country boy's life. And in other poems his later life, with its impassioned devotion to freedom and its lofty faith, is reflected as lucidly as his youth is in " Snow-Bound " and " The Barefoot Boy."

He himself was " the barefoot boy," and what Robert Burns said of himself Whittier might repeat : " The poetic genius of my country found me, as the prophetic bard Elijah did Elisha, at the plough, and threw her inspired mantle over me."

He was a farmer's son, born at a time when farm-life in New England was more frugal than it is now, and with no other heritage than the good name and example of parents and kinsmen, in whom simple virtues — thrift, industry, and piety — abounded.

His birthplace still stands near Haverhill, Mass., — a house in one of the hollows of the surrounding hills, little altered from what it was in 1807, the year he was born, when it was already at least a century and a half old.

He had no such opportunities for culture as Holmes and Lowell had in their youth. His parents were intelligent and upright people of limited means, who lived in all the simplicity of the Quaker faith, and there was nothing in his early surroundings to encourage and develop a literary taste. Books were scarce, and the twenty volumes on his father's shelves were about Quaker doctrines and Quaker heroes. There was one novel in the house, but it was hidden away, for fiction was forbidden fruit in that household. No library or scholarly companionship was within reach ; and if his gift had been less than genius it could never have triumphed over the many disadvantages it had to contend with. Instead of a poet, he would have been a farmer like his forefathers. But literature was a spontaneous impulse with him, as natural as the song of a bird, and he was not wholly dependent on training and opportunity as he would have been had he possessed mere talent.

Frugal from necessity, the life of the Whittiers was not sordid or cheerless to him, moreover, and he looks back to it as tenderly as if it had been full of luxuries. It was sweetened by strong affections, simple tastes, and an unflinching sense of duty, and in all the members of the household the love of nature was so genuine that meadow, wood, and river yielded them all the pleasure they needed, and they scarcely missed the refinements of art.

Surely there could not be a pleasanter or more homelike picture than that which the poet has given us of the family on the night of the great storm when the old house was snow-bound : —

> "Shut in from all the world without,
> We sat the clean-winged hearth about,
> Content to let the north-wind roar
> In baffled rage at pane and door,
> While the red logs before us beat
> The frost-line back with tropic heat ;
> And ever, when a louder blast
> Shook beam and rafter as it passed,
> The merrier up its roaring draught
> The great throat of the chimney laughed.

The house-dog on his paws outspread
Laid to the fire his drowsy head ;
The cat's dark silhouette on the wall
A couchant tiger's seemed to fall ;
And, for the winter fireside meet,
Between the andiron's straddling feet,
The mug of cider simmered slow,
The apples sputtered in a row,
And close at hand the basket stood
With nuts from brown October's wood."

The father was a plain, taciturn, yet prompt and decisive man, who in early life had explored the vast wilderness which extended from New Hampshire to Canada ; and sitting before the fire he told of his adventures : —

"Our father rode again his ride
On Memphremagog's wooded side ;
Sat down again to moose and samp
In trapper's hut or Indian camp."

The mother was a woman of gentle ways, much loved and honored in the neighborhood, with a low voice and a benign face.

"Our mother, while she turned her wheel,
Or run the new-knit stocking-heel.

Told how the Indian hordes came down
At midnight on Cocheco town,
And how her own great-uncle bore
His cruel scalp-marks to fourscore,
Recalling in her fitting phrase,
So rich and picturesque and free,
(The common unrhymed poetry
Of simple life and country ways,)
The story of her early days."

Her sister, Mercy Hussey, lived with the family, and, like Mrs. Whittier, wore the gray dress and white cap of the Quakers.

"The sweetest woman ever Fate
Perverse denied a household mate.

   .   .   .   .   .   .

Through years of toil and soil and care,
From glossy tress to thin gray hair,
All unprofaned she held apart
The virgin fancies of the heart."

The father's brother, Moses Whittier, also was a member of the family, — "a simple, guileless, childlike man," — and a great favorite, especially with the boys, as may be supposed from this picture: —

"Our uncle, innocent of books,
Was rich in lore of fields and brooks,
The ancient teachers, never dumb,
Of Nature's unhoused lyceum.

In moons and tides and weather wise,
He read the clouds as prophecies,
And foul or fair could well divine,
By many an occult hint or sign,
Holding the cunning-warded keys
To all the woodcraft mysteries.

.   .   .   .

He told how teal and loon are shot,
And how the eagle's eggs he got,
The feats on pond and river done,
The prodigies of rod and gun ;
Till, warming with the tales he told,
Forgotten was the outside cold,
The bitter wind unheeded blew ;
From ripening corn the pigeons flew,
The partridge drummed i' the wood, the mink
Went fishing down the river-brink ;
In fields with bean or clover gay,
The woodchuck, like a hermit gray,
Peered from the doorway of his cell ;
The muskrat plied the mason's trade,
And tier by tier his mud-walls laid ;
And from the shagbark overhead
The grizzled squirrel dropped his shell."

There were four children, two boys and
two girls.

"Our elder sister plied
Her evening task, the stand beside ;
A full, rich nature, free to trust,
Truthful, and almost sternly just,

Impulsive, earnest, prompt to act,
And make her generous thought a fact,
Keeping with many a light disguise
The secret of self-sacrifice.

. . . . . .

Upon the motley-braided mat
Our youngest and our dearest sat,
Lifting her large, sweet, asking eyes,
Now bathed within the fadeless green
And holy peace of Paradise."

For a picture of the poet himself, we must turn to the verses on "The Barefoot Boy" in which he says, —

" Oh for boyhood's time of June,
Crowding years in one brief moon,
When all things I heard or saw,
Me, their master, waited for !
I was rich in flowers and trees,
Humming-birds and honey-bees ;
For my sport the squirrel played,
Plied the snouted mole his spade ;
For my taste the blackberry cone
Purpled over hedge and stone ;
Laughed the brook for my delight
Through the day and through the night,
Whispering at the garden wall,
Talked with me from fall to fall ;
Mine the sand-rimmed pickerel pond,
Mine the walnut slopes beyond ;

> Mine, on bending orchard trees,
> Apples of Hesperides;
> Still, as my horizon grew,
> Larger grew my riches too:
> All the world I saw or knew
> Seemed a complex Chinese toy,
> Fashioned for a barefoot boy!"

The neighbors were as simple and as frugal as the Whittiers, though some of them were not so intelligent. They still believed in witches; and one night at a husking, when a big black bug came buzzing into the room, it was declared to be an old woman who was suspected of witchcraft. They struck at it, and knocked it down; and when on the next day the old woman was found ill in her cottage, they would not believe that the bruises with which she was covered had been received in a fall down stairs as she claimed, and insisted that they were the marks of the blows struck at the bug. Old Captain P——, who lived near her, and had a house and several barns, covered them all over with horse shoes to keep the witch out.

Their simplicity is shown by still another

story. A man was seen looking about in the woods with a gun, and gazing into all the bushes and up into the trees. At first they thought he was a lunatic, and then, deciding that he was a British spy, they had him arrested. The judge examined him and found out that his only business was shooting birds.

" Well," said the judge, " what do you do with them, — eat them ? "

" No."

" Do you sell them ? "

" No ; I study them."

He was a celebrated ornithologist, but the statement that he devoted all his time to studying birds was so incredible that he would have been sent to jail as a spy if he had not been able to prove his truthfulness by a letter from a Boston gentleman, which was in his possession.

There must have been some appeal to the imagination of a poetic youth in this mediæval *in*experience, and what charm there was in it Whittier certainly found. It is not his nature to complain, and there is no word of self-pity in all his works to show

that he was ever dissatisfied with his con-
dition in boyhood; but one cannot help
thinking that the budding poet, with his
delicate sensibilities and perceptions, must
have pined, now and then, for more books
and the conversation of scholars.

I doubt if any boy ever rose to intellectual eminence who had fewer opportunities
for education than Whittier. He had no
such pasturage to browse on as is open to
every reader, who, by simply reaching them
out, can lay his hands on the treasures
of English literature. He had to borrow
books wherever they could be found among
the neighbors who were willing to lend, and
he thought nothing of walking several miles
for one volume. The only instruction he
received was at the district school, which
was open a few weeks in midwinter, and at
the Haverhill Academy, which he attended
two terms of six months each, paying for
his tuition by work done in his spare
hours. A feeble spirit would have lan-
guished under such disadvantages, and
how he would have bewailed them after
outliving them! But Whittier scarcely re-

fers to them, and, instead of begging for
pity, he takes them as part of the common
lot, and seems to remember only what was
beautiful and good.

Occasionally a stranger knocked at the
door of the old homestead in the valley.
Sometimes it was a distinguished Quaker
from abroad, but oftener it was a pedler,
or some vagabond begging for food, which
was seldom refused. Once a foreigner
came, and asked for lodgings for the night,
— a dark, repulsive man, whose appearance
was so much against him that Mrs. Whittier was afraid to admit him. No sooner
had she sent him away, however, than she
repented. "What if a son of mine were in
a strange land!" she thought. The young
poet (who was not recognized as such)
offered to go out in search of him, and he
presently returned with him, having found
him standing in the roadway just as he had
been turned away from another house.

"He took his seat with us at the supper
table," says Whittier, in one of his prose
sketches, "and when we were all gathered
around the hearth that cold autumnal even-

ing, he told us, partly by words, partly by
gestures, the story of his life and misfortunes, amused us with descriptions of the
grape-gatherings and festivals of his sunny
clime, edified my mother with a receipt
for making bread of chestnuts, and in the
morning, when, after breakfast, his dark,
sullen face lighted up, and his fierce eye
moistened with grateful emotion as, in his
own silvery Tuscan accent, he poured out
his thanks, we marvelled at the fears which
had so nearly closed our doors against him,
and, as he departed, we all felt that he had
left with us the blessing of the poor."

This reads like a passage from the
" Vicar of Wakefield," and we are reminded
of the same book by the poet's description
of Jonathan Plummer, "maker of verses,
pedler and poet, physician and parson,"
who came twice a year to the Whittier
homestead. " He brought with him pins,
needles, tape, and cotton thread for my
mother; jack-knives, razors, and soap for
my father; and verses of his own composing, coarsely printed, and illustrated with
rude woodcuts, for the delectation of the

younger branches of the family. No love-
sick youth could drown himself, no deserted
maiden bewail the moon, no rogue mount
the gallows, without fitting memorial in
Plummer's verses. Earthquakes, fires, and
shipwrecks he regarded as personal favors
from Providence, furnishing the raw material of song and ballad. Welcome to us in
our country seclusion, as Autolycus to the
clown in ' A Winter's Tale,' we listened with
infinite satisfaction to his readings of his
own verses or to his ready improvisation
upon some dramatic incident or topic suggested by his auditors. . . . He was scru-
pulously conscientious, devout, inclined to
theological disquisitions, and withal mighty
in Scripture. He was thoroughly independent, flattered nobody, cared for nobody,
trusted nobody. When invited to sit down
at our dinner-table, he invariably took the
precaution to place his basket of valuables
between his legs for safe-keeping. ' Never
mind thy basket, Jonathan,' said my father,
' we sha'n't steal thy verses.' — ' I'm not sure
of that,' returned the suspicious guest; ' it
is written, "Trust ye not in any brother." ' "

Another guest came to the house one day. It was a vagrant old Scotchman, who, when he had been treated to bread and cheese and cider, sang some of the songs of Robert Burns, which Whittier then heard for the first time, and which he never forgot. Coming to him thus, as songs reached the people before printing was invented, through gleemen and minstrels, their sweetness lingered in his ears, and he soon found himself singing in the same strain. Some of his earliest inspiration was drawn from Burns, and he tells us of his joy, when, one day after the visit of the old Scotchman, his schoolmaster loaned him a copy of that poet's works. " I began to make rhymes myself, and to imagine stories and adventures," he says in his simple way.

Indeed, he began to rhyme almost as soon as he had learned to read, and he kept his gift a secret from all except his oldest sister, fearing that his father, who was a prosaic man, would think that he was wasting his time. He wrote under the fences, in the attic, in the barn, — wherever he could escape observation ; and, as pen and ink were not always available, he sometimes used chalk, and even charcoal. Great was the surprise of the family when some of his verses were unearthed — literally unearthed — from under a heap of rubbish in a garret. But his father frowned upon these evidences of the bent of his mind, not out of unkindness, but because he doubted the sufficiency of the boy's education for a literary life, and did not wish to inspire him with hopes which might never be fulfilled.

His sister had faith in him, nevertheless, and without his knowledge she sent one of his poems to the editor of the " Free Press," a newspaper published in Newburyport. Whittier was helping his father to repair a stone wall by the roadside, when the carrier flung a copy of the paper to him, and, unconscious that any thing of his own was in it, he opened it, and glanced up and down the columns. His eyes fell on some verses called " The Exile's Departure : " —

" Fond scenes which delighted my youthful existence,
    With feelings of sorrow I bid ye adieu, —
 A lasting adieu, for now, dim in the distance,
    The shores of Hibernia recede from my view.

Farewell to the cliffs, tempest-beaten and gray,
  Which guard the loved shores of my own native
    land !
Farewell to the village and sail-shadowed bay,
  The forest-crowned hill, and the water-washed
    strand ! "

His eyes swam. It was his own poem, — the first he ever had in print.

" What is the matter with thee ? " his father demanded, seeing how dazed he was ; but, though he resumed his work on the wall, he could not speak, and he had to steal a glance at the paper again and again before he could convince himself that he was not dreaming.

Sure enough, the poem was there with his initial at the foot of it, " W., Haverhill, June 1, 1826 ; " and, better still, this editorial notice : " If ' W.,' at Haverhill, will continue to favor us with pieces, beautiful as the one inserted in our poetical department of to-day, we shall esteem it a favor."

The editor thought so much of " The Exile's Departure " and some other verses which followed it from the same hand, that he resolved to make the acquaintance of

his new contributor, and he drove over to
see him.   Whittier, then a boy of eighteen,
was summoned from the fields where he
was working, clad only in shirt, trousers,
and straw hat; and having slipped in at
the back door, so that he might put his
shoes and coat on, came into the room
with "shrinking diffidence, almost unable
to speak, and blushing like a maiden."
The editor was a young man, not more
than twenty-two or twenty-three, and the
friendship that began with this visit lasted
until death ended it.   How strong and
close it was, and how it was made to serve
the cause of freedom, may be learned in
the life of the great abolitionist, William
Lloyd Garrison, for that was the editor's
name.

The poet's corner of the newspaper did
not prove to be the temple of fame which
Whittier imagined it to be when the " Free
Press " was dropped into his hands with his
poem in it, and he still had an up-hill path
before him.   But he was not consumed with
the desire for the glitter and noise which
satisfy some ambitions, and he lost thought

of himself in the great struggle for the emancipation of the negro which he joined with his friend Garrison. Fame never passes true genius by, however, and when it came it brought with it the love and reverence of thousands who recognize in Whittier a nature abounding in patience, unselfishness, and all the sweetness of Christian charity.

"Well" said Mrs Lecks "whether Mr Dusante comes back with two nieces, or a wife and daughter, or Mrs Dusante and a mother-in-law, or a pair of sisters, all we've got to say is: 'The board-money's in the ginger-jar' and let them do their worst."

From "The Casting away of Mrs Lecks and Mrs Aleshine"

Frank R. Stockton

April 7, 1888

FRANCIS RICHARD STOCKTON.

Mr. Stockton may be said to have been half a city boy and half a country boy, for his early years were divided between a life in town and a life in the country. He was born in Philadelphia, on April 5, 1834, and was one of twelve children, three of whom were by his father's first wife, and nine by a second wife. Six of the latter children survived to an adult age, and of these Frank was the first-born. His full name is Francis Richard Stockton, and he owes this, he tells us, to the romantic tastes of one of his half-sisters, who insisted on his being called Francis after the first King of France, who bore that name, and Richard after Richard the Lion-hearted, King of England.

When he was ten years old, his family moved from Philadelphia to a farmhouse in Bucks County, Penn., and, as no school was within reach, he and his brothers were allowed to run wild, and to amuse themselves in the various ways that were sure to occur to high-spirited and healthy boys when left to their own resources.

Nothing that Mr. Stockton has written is more amusing than the story of his own boyhood, as I have had the privilege of hearing him tell it.

The house in Bucks County was one of the most fascinating places in the world for a boy. It was near the woods, where game could be found; neighbors were few and far between; and about a mile away there was a wild tract called Green Swamp, to which all sorts of awe-inspiring legends attached. It was said to be impenetrable to man, though haunted by strange beasts; and in the middle of it was a upas-tree, which, like that of the fable, stifled all things that came near it. The rumored impenetrability of the swamp, and the legend of the upas, made it all the more inviting to the boys, of course, and they attempted again and again to explore it. The water and bog were dotted with hummocks of solid land, like plums in a pudding, and they had to leap from one to the other of these. Sometimes they slipped, and got soaked in the ooze, but they were never able to get very far, and whether the upas is there or not is still a mystery.

Somewhere under the roof of the house there was an apartment which was called the gun-room, — probably to distinguish it from the other rooms, rather than from its use as the family arsenal. Exploring this one day, Francis the First and Richard the Lion-hearted, united in the small and mischievous person commonly called Frank, found an old gun without a lock, which had been condemned as useless. The idea of condemning a gun merely because it had no lock, struck him as a piece of folly; it was easy to repair so slight a defect as that. So he loaded the gun, and took it out with him into the garden, carrying an ordinary hammer with him as he went. He put a percussion-cap on the nipple, and having rested his weapon on the frame of a hot-bed in the garden, — for it was a heavy old blunderbuss, — he took aim at a neighbor's chickens, and then struck the cap with the hammer in his hand. The gun went off, and three of the chickens fell. For a moment his experiment seemed to have been an unqualified success, but there was a stinging sensation near his eye. The cap had flown off the nipple, and struck him, and he nearly lost his sight. This was one of the many lessons he had, that it is not wise to assume that one's elders are all fools.

The boys slept in a great, old-fashioned, four-post bed, and one night they turned it over, and climbed up into the high plat- form which it made when inverted. They were within a few inches of the ceiling, and they proposed to sleep in this way ; but their mother was brought to the scene by the noise they had made, and they had to replace the bed in its proper position.

They told stories after they went to bed, Frank and his brother John collaborating for the amusement of their younger brother William, who lay at the foot of the bed. Frank would start the story, and at the point where he left off, John would take it up, depending on his own imagination for the continuation. The end was often very different from what the beginner had intended it to be ; but the uncertainty of the development quickened the interest, both for the narrator and the listener, who, if he dared to go to sleep during the story, was immediately kicked out of bed.

Frank was small, and rather slight of figure, but he was as athletic as the rest. They were all good riders and swimmers, and were fond of gardening and carpentry. Their knack in the latter was remarkable. They used the full-sized tools of a working carpenter, and built houses which, though not fitted for human occupation, would have been too large for any doll but one of extravagant tastes.

At the end of three years their parents decided that the untrammelled life the boys were leading would not do any longer, and they returned to Philadelphia. Frank had already been in a private school, and he was now sent to a public school, from which he passed into the Central High

School. He was graduated with the degree of Bachelor of Arts.

He was not an ambitious boy, but a clever one, and it was easy for him to stand second in his class. His natural bent was in the direction of literature, and he was not more than ten years old when he began to write verses. On one occasion he sent a poem to a religious paper published in Baltimore, and when it was returned to him he made up his mind that the editor was an ignorant person, who could not appreciate a good thing, and who would have rejected the works of Shakspeare and Milton had they been offered to him. To prove this point, he copied out one of Milton's devotional poems, and, having attached a fictitious name to it, he sent it to the same editor. He was chagrined to find, however, that the editor at once recognized its merits and printed it, though he, this arbiter of the destiny of literary aspirants, did not detect the fictitious character of the alleged author.

The restraints of the city did not curb

the frolicsome propensities of Frank and
his brothers. Their father was a devout
man, who frequently entertained the minis-
ters of his denomination; and one day,
when some of these gentlemen were guests
at dinner, it was noticed with surprise that
all the boys refused mince-pie. They
seemed to be choking, and rushed away
from the table when it was offered to them.
The pie had been made the evening before,
and during the night the boys had stolen
into the pantry, and substituted mush for
the mince-meat. They had many a clan-
destine supper in their night-dresses, and
used to slide down the banisters, because,
as one of their number impressed upon
them (very likely it was Frank), the crack-
ing of their knees would perhaps have
awakened the household.

They had a secret society, and when a
candidate presented himself for admission,
this question was asked him: "If your
mother was being chased by an Indian who
wanted to tomahawk her, and she hid her-
self in some place that you knew of, what
would you say to the Indian if he asked

you where she was?" If the candidate admitted that he would deceive the Indian under such circumstances as these, he was considered worthy of admission, but if he said his adherence to truth would compel him to sacrifice his mother to the savage, he was rejected.

They also belonged to another society, the Crazy Club, of which Frank was the chief officer, his title being the Grand Worthy Maniac. The meetings of the club were held in boats on the river, and the Grand Worthy Maniac exercised a despotic authority over the members. They were required to obey his mandates implicitly, and he would sometimes order one of them to take off his clothes, and swim, on a moonlight night, into the middle of the stream, and sing comic songs while floating there.

Once they ventured to play at pirates, and rowed out in chase of another boat which some boys were pulling. The latter did not seem in the least alarmed, nor did they make any attempt to avoid capture. When they were overtaken, the pirate chief

demanded, " What do you mean by coming
out on this river?" But they made no
answer, and showed no intention of resist-
ance. This nonplussed the pursuers, who
had imagined that there would be a hand-
to-hand combat, in which they would be
the victors. " What do you mean?" they
repeated. Still the other boys had nothing
to say; and instead of making them walk
the plank as they had intended, the pirates
rowed off very quietly, saying, " Now, never
do it again, that's all." Piracy did not
seem to be as exciting as some stories
made it appear.

Behind all this nonsense and mischief
there was plenty of hard work and solid
reading. Frank was graduated from the
Central High School when he was eighteen
years old, and was intended to be a physician ; but, for some unexplained reason, he
took up the art of wood-engraving. His
ambition was to be an author, and he gave
his leisure to writing articles and stories,
many of which were accepted and printed
while he was still a boy. Then he gave
up wood-engraving altogether, and entered

on a journalistic career, which, when " St. Nicholas" was started, in 1873, led him into the position of assistant editor of that attractive magazine, under the editorship of Mrs. Mary Mapes Dodge.   Long before this he had made a reputation as a humorous and fanciful writer, but it was not until he was forty years old, or more, that he made his greatest hit with the Rudder Grange stories, in which the rare quality of his genius was first discovered.   Thirteen years have gone by, each year bringing him some new honor, and he does not look a day older now than he did then. He still looks like a man of thirty-five, and he may be considered an instance of what he terms " protracted youth."

A Mother's Picture —

She seemed an angel to our infant eyes!
Once, when the glorifying moon revealed
Her who at evening by our pillow kneeled,—
Soft-voiced and golden-haired, from holy skies
Flown to her loves on wings of Paradise,—
We looked to see the pinions half-concealed.
The Tuscan vines and olives will not yield
Her back to me, who loved her in this wise
And since have little known her, but have grown
To see another mother tenderly
Watch over sleeping children of my own.
Perchance the years have changed her: yet alone
This picture lingers; still she seems to me
The fair young angel of my infancy.

1860
1858

Edmund C. Stedman —

EDMUND CLARENCE STEDMAN.

LET the reader picture to himself an old man in such a costume as a prosperous lawyer would wear forty years ago, with a defiant boy standing before him. The old man is reproving, and the boy has not yet been reduced to the point of penitence.

"Come, sir," says the elder severely, wishing to show that the culprit's offence is without a parallel, "did you ever hear of any great man who ran away from home in his youth?"

"Yes," the boy blurts out to the surprise of his questioner.

"And who was it, pray?"

"Masterman Ready, sir."

"Masterman Ready" is not a name to be found in dictionaries of illustrious person ages, but to the imaginative boy Capt. Marryat's hero seemed to afford a very good precedent in justification of his conduct.

The old man's sense of humor was touched; and for some time afterwards — long enough for him to see the folly of his excuse — the boy was nicknamed " Masterman Ready."

His real name was Edmund Clarence Stedman; and his Mentor was his great-uncle, James Stedman of Norwich, Conn., who was bringing him up.

Though born in Hartford, Conn., he was taken while an infant to Plainfield, N.J.; and in his sixth year, when his mother, who had been widowed, married a second time, he was transferred to the care of this uncle at Norwich, where he remained until he reached the age of fifteen.

It was Norwich Town, two miles away from the city of Norwich; a quaint old place not unlike Portsmouth, full of colonial houses, and historic families like the Huntingtons, the Trumbulls, and the Stedmans themselves. It was the birthplace of Benedict Arnold. Old traditions were believed in, and old customs observed. No town in New England celebrated Thanksgiving as Norwich Town did. Enor-

mous bonfires were burned, such as reduced ordinary bonfires to glow-worms by
comparison; barrels strung on masts sixty
feet high, begged or bought by gangs of
boys in the surrounding neighborhood for
months before. A capital place for any
boy, one would say, and especially for a boy
of an imaginative turn of mind with a taste
for romance.

There were six boys in the house of
James Stedman, so that there was no lack
of companionship; and a curious thing
about these six boys was that they were
three pairs of brothers, the elder of each
pair being two years the senior of the
younger, while the respective ages of each
pair were alike; or, in other words, the
eldest of one pair was the same age as
the eldest of the other pairs, and the age
of the youngest was the same in each case
also. There was not a place for berrying
or nutting that they did not know, nor was
there an adventure in which they did not
unite. And at night, when they reached
home, they sat up in bed telling stories; and
in this amusement, as in their expeditions

in the woods, Edmund Clarence Stedman was the leader.

A small, active, sinewy little fellow he was, of a slender frame but great endurance, sensitive, impulsive, passionate ; and though he was what may be called an out-of-door boy, rejoicing in physical exercises, — a good swimmer, a champion runner, and expert in woodcraft, into the mysteries of which he was initiated by a half-breed named Ira, — he was as eager for learning as for sport, and he stood at the head of his class in the Norwich Academy.

But despite his vitality he was not a happy boy. He had all the painful sensibilities of the poetic temperament, and often withdrew from companionship to be alone with his own thoughts. His great-uncle was a disciplinarian, a just, well-meaning but exacting man, quite incapable, apparently, of understanding the ultimate value of the fiery and imaginative character of his nephew, though he was of the greatest use to the latter in his studies, and found in him such a pupil as a thorough-going scholar loves.

Except in their love of learning they had little in common, however, and the boy rebelled against the ascetic life around him, and that bitter sectarian feeling which ran so high in Norwich Town that the young people of one denomination were forbidden to play with those of other churches. Then — and this was the principal source of his unhappiness — he was separated from his mother, and to a boy of his temperament no deprivation could be more serious than this. How pitifully his soul yearned for her through all the years he spent in Norwich Town! How in every moment of despair it seemed that only her presence was needed to make him happy, and set him right! How clearly she would have been able to see what all the rest misunderstood! He was much like her in his tastes, and he had inherited from her a love of poets and poetry which deepened the sympathy between them. She did nor discourage or disparage the poetic faculty, as parents often wisely do. "My son, be a poet," she said, and he hardly needed her direction, for he had begun to rhyme in infancy.

Scott, Coleridge, Shelley, Keats, and Byron cast the spell of their genius over him, and lightened the burdens of many of his weary hours.

At the age of fifteen he went to Yale, with the largest class that ever entered that college, — a class, too, that was notable for its literary ability. George W. Smalley (" G. W. S."), the London correspondent of the "Tribune;" Andrew D. White, afterwards president of Cornell University; Isaac H. Bromley, Charlton T. Lewis, and Delano Goddard, the latter three all journalists of wide reputation, — were among the members.

Here he distinguished himself by his Greek and English compositions, and took a first prize in his sophomore year. But he did not remain to graduate, though in after years the college placed him among its alumni with the degree of M.A. He wanted to see the world, and he set out in search of adventure, on an expedition which ended with less romantic results than he expected.

He wavered between the choice of literature and journalism, but the latter seemed to offer the more solid ground; and one day when he was in New York he sought an audience with Horace Greeley, who was his ideal of a great editor. Mr. Greeley sat in an armchair, reading a paper, while a shoe-black was polishing his shoes, a luxury to which, it is said, the famous journalist did not often treat himself. The boy approached timidly and reverently, and inquired whether there was any vacancy on the staff. "No, young man," was the curt reply, and this one word closed the interview as a shutter extinguishes a dancing sunbeam. The novice had been in the presence of his hero, however, and the brief speech lingered in his ear as if it had been a burst of eloquence.

The poetic quality was not an enfeebling trait in this youth. He had fine courage and manly resolution. He went back to Norwich, and at nineteen became the editor of the Norwich "Tribune," engaging his old classmate, Isaac H. Bromley, to assist him. Then he took charge of the " Herald," published at Winsted, Conn., imparting to it a dignity and an originality which country newspapers do not usually have; and a year or two later he removed to New York, where, after a while, he found the vacancy on Horace Greeley's staff for which he had been looking.

He went to the front as war correspondent, and showed all the courage, endurance, and fertility of resource, which that post requires. Had he chosen, he might have filled the highest positions in journalism; but literature in the form of poetry and criticism had a greater attraction for him, and his work in this direction has revealed the unusual combination of creative imagination and dispassionate judgment. All sorts of honors have come to him, but he remains a boy in the earnestness of his friendships and the freshness of his enthusiasms. His mother is an idol still, and of her he has written in one of his poems, —

" She seemed an angel to our infant eyes !
    Once when the glorifying moon revealed
    Her who at evening by our pillow kneeled, —
  Soft-voiced and golden-haired, from holy skies
  Flown to her loves on wings of Paradise, —

We looked to see the pinions half concealed.
The Tuscan vines and olives will not yield
Her back to me, who loved her in this wise,
And since have little known her, but have grown
To see another mother tenderly
Watch over sleeping children of my own.
Perhaps the years have changed her : yet alone
This picture lingers ; still she seems to me
The fair young angel of my infancy."

EDWARD EVERETT HALE.

THE boyhood of Edward Everett Hale reads like a chapter in one of his own stories of home life. There was nothing miraculous or romantic in it; no prodigious feats of learning, no martyrdom, and no canonization of saints.

His father and mother were just the kind of people that he holds up to admiration in his books, — full of good sense, liberality, and originality; controlling their children with a secure hand, but directing instead of driving them, and reasoning with them instead of scolding. Piety in that household never wore a long face ; benevolence worked in deeds and not in words.

At the end of his first month in the Boston Latin School, the boy came home with a report which showed that he was ninth in a class of fifteen ; and he dreaded handing it to his mother, as he thought she would be displeased to find him so low

Dear Sir:-

I am greatly obliged
to you, and look for-
ward with much inter-
est to the articles-

Truly yours

Edward E. Hale

in the class. "Oh," she said, "that is
no matter. Probably the other boys are
brighter than you. God made them so,
and you cannot help that. But the report
says that you are among the boys who behave well. That you can see to, and that
is all I care about."

This little incident shows the reasona-
bleness which guided the conduct of the
Hale household. A boy was expected to
do all in his power, but no more ; and if
he could not do it one way, he was allowed
to attempt it by some new method, which
often proved to be no less successful on
account of its novelty. He was not forced
to conform to patterns, simply because they
fitted other boys, though there was no lack
of discipline and no toleration of the wilful
misuse of time. The motto that has since
become famous was so closely lived up to,
that it might have been as unceasingly in
the ears of the family as the ticking of the
clock : —

"Look up, and not down ;
Look forward, and not back ;
Look out, and not in ;
Lend a hand."

The boy who was born in Boston on April 3, 1822, came of a stock which justified the expectation of a brilliant and useful career for him. His grand-uncle was Nathan Hale, who, when he was led out to execution as a spy in the Revolutionary war, said with his last breath, "I regret that I have only one life to surrender for my country;" and his uncle on his mother's side was Edward Everett the orator, after whom he was named. His father was a man who combined scholarship with activity in public affairs, and it was through his advocacy that the first steam railway was built in Massachusetts.

Great are the changes that have taken place in Boston since then. The boy is a man, and looking back says, "I have sailed my bark boat on the salt waters, where I now can sit in the parlors of my parishioners. I have studied botany on the marshes, where I now sit in my own study to prepare the notes which I read to you. I rode in triumph on the locomotive which hissed over the first five miles that were ready of that highway to

the West, where now she might run five
thousand."

A good half of Boston is built on land
recovered from the sea; and there are
solid streets and houses where, less than
half a century ago, the water flowed, sink-
ing and rising with the tides.

He was sent to a dame-school while he
was still an infant; but he learned little
there, and probably was not expected to
learn. As the children droned through
their lessons, he sat quietly watching the
motes of dust dancing in the sunbeams
that streamed through the blinds, and his
greatest interest was in the making of
sand-pies on the floor. When he was
placed in a big yellow chair in the middle
of the room, he could not be made to understand that it was for some misconduct.

Then he was sent to a school kept by
a man who was amiable but incompetent,
and he gathered scarcely more here than
he did in watching the sunbeams. "A
feather-pillow sort of a man was 'Simple'
the master, — a good-natured, innocent
fellow, who would neither set the bay on

fire nor want to, who could and would keep us out of mischief for five or six hours a day, and would never send us home mad with rage, or injustice, or ambition."

He was sometimes late in coming to school; and in order to reproach him, Edward Everett Hale, then a small and audacious lad, marshalled all the boys in their seats, and had a class out to recite before he arrived.

This saucy boy had strong opinions on many subjects at this early age, and he put little value on schools and schoolmasters. But he was a great reader, and his reading fertilized his mind as a field is fertilized before the sower scatters the seed.

Grimm's " Fairy Stories " opened the world of magic to him ; and the poems of Sir Walter Scott had such a fascination for him, that there never was a time after he had read them, when he could not quote long passages from memory. As with all imaginative boys, a book of travels transported him to the very spot described ; and as he read an account of the Arctic regions, the house melted into air, and he seemed to be sitting in the cabin of an ice-bound ship, held fast in the jaws of the polar sea, with the aurora flashing up and down the sky. Happy is the boy whose imagination has such a spread of wing that he can leave every care on earth behind, and forget himself in a book! Life has no greater boon than this, and it is the special gift of youth which age can seldom claim.

When he was nine years of age he was sent to the Boston Latin School, where Benjamin Franklin, Samuel Adams, John Hancock, Edward Everett, and Charles Sumner had been educated. It is the oldest school in America, and one of the best; and in it the subject of our sketch made substantial progress, though he seldom stood higher than ninth in a class of fifteen. Unlike most budding authors, he was fond of arithmetic; and another peculiarity of his was, that he could not for the life of him see why his opinions on matters of education were not regarded with as much consideration as the master's. "I had a very decided feeling that it was as fitting that he should consult me as I him," he says with charming frankness.

All the while he was reading diligently; and two summers he was taken out of school to read at home, an excellent plan when a boy is growing fast, though it would be a pity if he should miss the hardening and sharpening which come from association with other boys.

Another privilege he had which any boy who aspires to become an author or a journalist might well envy. Who that is stirred with such an ambition has not looked up with awe and longing, to the front of a great newspaper-office, wishing that he might be admitted to its secrets, its labors, and its honors? Nothing in the world has seemed so glorious, not even the Capitol, pillars, steps, dome, and all, as a newspaper-building in some by-street of the city, with its lights shining in the upper story where the compositors are setting type, the presses rattling in the basement, and the entrance with editors, reporters, and messengers coming and going at all hours of the day and night.

Well, the father of Edward Everett Hale
was the editor of the Boston "Advertiser," and the offices of that paper resembled a nursery to his son, who, like William Dean Howells, learned to set type
almost as soon as he had learned to read.
He not only mastered the mechanical parts
of the business of making a newspaper,
but wrote articles for the "Advertiser"
while he was still a boy, and he translated
an article from a French paper for it
before he was eleven: a good beginning
for one who in after-life was to fill in turn
every position, from that of a reporter, to
the much loftier perch of the controlling
editor.

In 1835 he entered Harvard University,
where Lowell was already a student; and
his literary tastes were fostered there by
Edward Tyrrel Channing, the professor of
English language and literature, who also
taught Dana, Story, Holmes, Parkman,
and many others who have since made
their mark in authorship. Longfellow was
another of the professors. "He came to
Cambridge in our first years. He was not

so much older than we as to be distant, was always accessible, friendly, and sympathetic. All poor teachers let the book come between them and the pupil. Great teachers never do : Longfellow never did. We used to call him ' Head,' which meant head of the modern language department."

Hale was graduated in 1839, and about that time he made the acquaintance of two new authors through their books. One was Alfred Tennyson, and the other John Ruskin. The first copy of Tennyson that fell into his hands had been brought from England by Emerson, who was always kind to young people, and lent his books freely. Then Ruskin appeared, and his writings developed the love of the beautiful in the young student, and gave him the habit of a close observation of nature out of doors. Scarcely any thing in the shape of a book was uninteresting or unprofitable to him ; but he confesses that he could not enjoy Locke's " Essay on the Human Understanding," and that he went to sleep over it.

After his graduation, he taught Latin and

Greek for two years, and at the same time wrote articles and stories for the papers. He is as widely known now as an author as he is as a preacher; but when he was twenty-four he entered the Christian ministry, and he has never given it up. The best of his endeavors have been devoted to it, and in his life he has been governed by a principle which he uttered before a college society, — " We professional men must serve the world, not, like the handicraftsman, for a price accurately representing the work done ; but as those who deal with infinite values, and confer benefits as freely and nobly as Nature."

JAMES RUSSELL LOWELL.

Some winter's evening, when the reader
of this is in a mood to beguile himself with
a pleasant book of essays, I would advise
him to take down from the shelf the " Fireside Travels " of James Russell Lowell, in
which he will find among other good things
a picturesque account of Cambridge as it
was in the poet's boyhood. " Cambridge
Thirty Years Ago " he calls it, but the time
he describes has crept back twenty years
more since it was written, and to us it is
a picture, not of thirty years, but of half a
century, ago.

Cambridge was not the noisy and populous place then that it is now. It was not
linked to Boston by the endless chain of
horse-cars which are running to and fro
night and day. It was a quiet country
village, resembling the country villages of
England, and resting in the shade of wide-

12ᵗʰ Feb: 1890.

Dear Mr Wingate,

I remember your name & your visit, & thank you for the kind things you are good enough to say. They were very grateful to me.

I have found comfort, I should rather say sustainment in the Book of Job (I could hardly explain why) & in the triumphant passages of the Burial Service in the English Liturgy — some of which are taken from Job. At one dark period of my life (but this is between ourselves) I recited this Service every morning before leaving my chamber. This I did for a year, & found it helpful. I then abandoned it

C. F. Wingate, Esqⁿ

because I found it gradually becoming mechanical. I have found sympathy too in such poems as Bishop King's "Gregory," & Henry Vaughan's "They are all gone into a world of light", but I never met with any "Collection" that I cared for & should think a good one might be useful.

Faithfully yours

J. R. Lowell

I wonder that I forgot Donne. Some of his poems — his "Anniversaries", for instance, — are full of food for sorrow, or it is that we want more than consolation which can't be had in any Poems.

branched, thick-leaved elms, lindens, and horse-chestnuts. The Revolution was as fresh in the public mind as the Civil War is to-day; and the recent presence of the British soldiers could be traced in the hooks from which they had hung their hammocks, and in the dents made by their muskets on the floor of the minister's library in the old gambrel-roofed house where the picture of a lady was shown with a slit in the canvas, which a red-coat had made with a thrust of his rapier.

People were still living who remained loyal to King George; and women still washed clothes in the town spring. One coach carried all the passengers there were between the village and Boston. A youth named Oliver Wendell Holmes, who had just gone forth from the gambrel-roofed house to study medicine in the schools of Paris, was spoken of as a sprightly versifier, who might make his mark in literature if he chose. The poetical accomplishments of another young man named Longfellow had been heard of in the community, though he had not yet been invited to take a professorship in the college as he was a few years later. Ralph Waldo Emerson was preaching in Boston, and John Greenleaf Whittier, a young Quaker of Haverhill, was filling an editor's chair, and sending out verses that thrilled with the promise of genuine lyric feeling.

Though he was destined to become their intimate in after-years, Lowell knew none of these at this time. They had all begun the battle of life, while he was still a schoolboy, with his hands in his pockets, and his eyes open to all the sights of the little world around him.

" Everybody knew everybody, and all about everybody," he says in " Fireside Travels ; " " and village wit, whose high 'change was around the little market-house in the town square, had labelled every more marked individuality with nicknames that clung like burs." There was the village whitewasher, all of whose belongings emblemized his trade. He whitewashed his trees, and grew the whitest of china asters in his garden. He wore a white neckcloth; and kept white fowls,

white ducks, and white geese. There was
an old Scotch gardener who told romantic
stories, and showed an imaginary French
bullet, sometimes in one leg, sometimes in
the other, and sometimes toward nightfall
in both. One of the two grocers was a
deacon, upon whom the boys were fond of
playing a familiar joke.

One of them would enter the shop, and
ask, " Have you any sour apples, deacon ? "

" Well, no, I haven't any just now that
are exactly sour ; but there's the bell-flower
apple, and folks that like a sour apple generally like that."

Another boy would then come in, and
say, " Have you any sweet apples, deacon ? "

" Well, no," the deacon would reply, " I
haven't any just now that are exactly sweet ;
but there's the bell-flower apple, and folks
that like a sweet apple generally like that."

Thus it was that the deacon's apples
were suited to the customer's taste, whether
he wanted them sour or sweet.

The barber's shop was a sort of museum,
and no boy ever went there to have his

hair cut that he was not accompanied by troops of friends, who thus inspected the curiosities gratis.

"What a charming place it was, how full of wonder and delight!" says Lowell in the essay already quoted. "The sunny little room, fronting south-west upon the common, rang with canaries and Java sparrows, nor were the familiar notes of robin, thrush, and bobolink wanting; and a large white cockatoo harangued vaguely at intervals, in what we believed on R., the barber's, authority to be the Hottentot language. . . . The walls were covered with curious old Dutch prints, beaks of albatross and penguin, and whales' teeth fantastically engraved. There was Frederick the Great, with head drooped plottingly, and keen sidelong glance from under the three-cornered hat. There hung Bonaparte, too, the long-haired, haggard general of Italy, his eyes sombre with prefigured destiny; and there was his silent grave, — the dream and the fulfilment. Good store of sea-fights there was also; above all, Paul Jones in the ' Bonhomme Richard,' the

smoke rolling courteously to leeward, that
we might see him dealing thunderous work
to the two hostile vessels, each twice as
large as his own, and the reality of the
scene corroborated by streaks of red paint
leaping from the mouth of every gun.
Suspended over the fireplace, with the
curling-tongs, were an Indian bow and
arrows ; and in the corners of the room
stood New Zealand paddles and war-clubs,
quaintly carved. The model of a ship in
glass we variously estimated to be worth
from a hundred to a thousand dollars —
the barber rather favoring the higher valu-
ation, though never distinctly committing
himself. Among these wonders, the only
suspicious one was an Indian tomahawk,
which had too much the peaceful look of a
shingling-hatchet. Did any rarity enter
the town, it gravitated naturally to these
walls, to the very nail that waited to receive
it, and where, the day after its accession, it
seemed to have hung a lifetime."

Lowell's home was at Elmwood, about a
mile away from Harvard Square, and it
was in this roomy mansion that he was

born on Feb. 22, 1819. His father was a Unitarian clergyman, and he was descended from a long line of prosperous people who had originally come to America from Bristol, Eng. The city of Lowell was named after one of them, and another was the founder of the Lowell Institute in Boston, an educational establishment to which he left two hundred and fifty thousand dollars by a will written while he was on the summit of the Great Pyramid.

The house is still screened from the highway by the giant trees around it, though the jingle of the horse-cars and the rumble of passing carriages and carts now jar upon its quiet; but when the poet was a boy it was in a solitude, and the only noises were the cries of the birds which thronged the garden.

He was fond of birds, as the reader can well believe who knows an essay of his called "My Garden Acquaintance;" and the feathered visitors who came to Elmwood and gossiped in its cavernous shade were always treated as welcome guests. There were robins, catbirds, blue-jays,

orioles, bobolinks, blackbirds, and herons.
What could be better than Lowell's description of the robins?

"They are feathered Pecksniffs, to be
sure; but then how brightly their breasts,
that look rather shabby in the sunlight,
shine in a rainy day against the dark
green of the fringe-tree! After they have
pinched and shaken all the life out of an
earth-worm, as Italian cooks pound all the
spirit out of a steak, and then gulped him,
they stand up in honest self-confidence, ex-
pand their red waistcoats with the virtuous
air of a lobby member, and outface you
with an eye that calmly challenges inquiry.
' Do *I* look like a bird that knows the
flavor of raw vermin? I throw myself
upon a jury of my peers. Ask any robin
if he ever ate any thing less ascetic than
the frugal berry of the juniper, and he will
answer that his vow forbids him!' Can
such an open bosom cover such depravity?
Alas, yes! I have no doubt his breast was
redder at that very moment with the blood
of my raspberries. On the whole, he is a
doubtful friend in the garden. He makes

his dessert of all kinds of berries, and is not averse from early pears. But when we remember how omnivorous he is, eating his own weight in an incredibly short time, and that Nature seems exhaustless in her inventions of new insects hostile to vegetation, perhaps we may reckon that he does more good than harm. For my own part, I would rather have his cheerfulness and kind neighborhood than many berries."

The birds returned the friendship of the inmates of the house with unwonted confidence, and would sometimes fly through the hall or the library. But, though the boy had so much interest in them, he never "oologized" them, and if they would not come near for him to observe them, he brought them closer with an opera-glass — a much better weapon, as he says, than a gun.

No school can ever do as much for a sensitive boy as the influence and example of parents of scholarly tastes, with whom the habit of reading is as regular as eating or sleeping. Lowell's father was a scholar,

and his mother, as well, was a person of
liberal culture and literary capacity, who,
as soon as her children could read, opened
to them the treasures of English literature, —

> " The old melodious lays
> Which softly melt the ages through,
> The songs of Spenser's golden days,
> Arcadian Sidney's silvery phrase."

Chaucer, Shakspeare, and Milton were
familiar to them at an age when most children are still reciting nursery rhymes; and
in James Russell Lowell, who was the
youngest of them, the influence of these
masters struck with deeper roots than in
the others, bringing forth in good time a
fruit of its own.

Elmwood was full of books, and they
were not allowed to lie dusty and unused
on the shelves. Access to them under the
direction of as discriminating a student as
Mrs. Lowell was in itself an education;
but it was not deemed to be enough, and
the young poet was sent to a classical
school in the neighborhood, where he was
prepared for Harvard College.

What sort of a boy was he at this time?
A letter from one of his classmates, the
Hon. G. B. Loring, lies open before the
writer of these lines: " He was a rapid
reader, and had a keen appreciation of all
noble thoughts, and a deep sympathy with
all noble characters. He learned his lessons with great ease, but was not fond
of mathematics, though he comprehended
readily philosophical theories. He loved
poetry, and his own faculty of versification
was notable even then. He had decided
political views, and was a Whig in those
days of Whiggery and Democracy, because
he thought the latter a pretence, and not
the embodiment of doctrines accordant
with the name. He was by nature devout
and conservative in his religious views, and
he was an advocate of temperance obliga-
tions as a safeguard against temptation.
Perhaps he did not set an example of
intense application, but he acquired knowledge more easily than many of his fellows.
His wit flashed about in a way which sometimes startled the dull, and always whetted
the edge of the bright; but he was a boy

without malice, and with strong attach-
ments, a dutiful son, and a devoted friend.
His tastes were simple, and free from all
desire for display. Although at times subject to those moods which fall upon boys
as well as men who have sensitive natures,
he struggled alone through his cloudy hours,
and gave only his sunshine to his friends."

He was a brilliant letter-writer, and his
private correspondence was sprinkled with
verses, many of which have never been
published. Mr. Loring has a bundle of
such letters from him, in which prose is
often dropped for a cantering rhyme. In
one, describing an early trip to the White
Mountains, he writes : —

> " I suppose you remember when Time was young ;
>   Say ! What made him so crabbed and cross?
> Did he speculate largely in Eastern lands,
>   Which the deluge made all a dead loss?
> Did he lose his affianced (poor soul) in the flood?
>   Or write a small poem or two,
> And turn misanthropic on reading a squib
>   In some acid pre-Adam Review?"

Again, answering his friend, a student
of medicine, who had tried his hand at a

verse or two, as a tribute to his genius, he
wrote : —

> " Dear friend and true, I take your hand,
>   A hand I love to clasp,
> And welcome you to Muse's land
>   With warm and hearty grasp.
> Not that you need a welcome there,
>   For what you wrote to me
> Would justly claim a right to wear
>   The wreath of poesy.
> But I dare trust that smile of mine
>   Will never come amiss,
> Although it scarce may hope to shine
>   Through fog-verse such as this.
> You have more legal right than I
>   To build the lofty rhyme,
> (Though when my shingle shines on high
>   I may enjoy more time),
> For Esculapius was the son
>   Of golden-haired Apollo,
> And if you win the heart of one,
>   The other's sure to follow."

Lowell entered Harvard in his sixteenth
year, and he has said of himself that he
read every thing except the text-books pre-
scribed by the Faculty. He was graduated
in the class of 1838, and then entered the
Law School, intending, like Oliver Wendell
Holmes, to become a lawyer. He even
went so far as to open a law-office in

Boston, but it is more than suspected that one of his early attempts at fiction, bearing the title of " My First Client," referred to an entirely imaginary person. " The old melodious lays" were still more fascinating to him than the law-books bound up in yellow sheepskin, and his circumstances were so easy that he was not forced to con- tinue work that was distasteful to him.

He published a little book of verse, and when he was twenty-four he started a magazine ; but, though neither the book nor the magazine met with success, he soon afterwards proved that by the closing of the little office and Blackstone's Com- mentaries, literature had gained more than law had lost.

Elmwood is still the home of Mr. Lowell when he is in the United States, and though many of the birds have now disappeared, the herons which lingered in its shade were made the subject of one of Longfellow's last poems : —

" Warm and still is the summer night,
  As here by the river's brink I wander,
White overhead the stars, and white
  The glimmering lamps on the hillside yonder.

" Silent are all the sounds of day ;
    Nothing I hear but the chirp of crickets,
And the cry of the herons winging their way
    O'er the poet's house in the Elmwood thickets.

" Call to him, herons, as slowly you pass
    To your roosts in the haunts of the exiled thrushes ;
Sing him the song of the green morass,
    And the tides that water the reeds and rushes.

          .   .   .   .

" Sing to him, say to him, here at his gate,
    Where the boughs of the stately elms are meeting,
Some one hath lingered to meditate,
    And send him unseen this friendly greeting ;

"That many another hath done the same,
    Though not by a sound was the silence broken :
The surest pledge of a deathless name
    Is the silent homage of thoughts unspoken."

Evolution.

I am the child of earth & air & sea!
My lullaby by hoarse Silurian storms
Was chanted; & through endless changing forms
Of plant & bird & beast unceasingly
The toiling ages wrought to fashion me.
Lo, these large ancestors have left a breath
Of their strong souls in mine, defying
And doom. I grow & blossom as the tree
And never feel deep-delving earthy roots
Binding me daily to the common clay;
But with its airy impulse upward shoots
My life into the realms of light & day;
And thou, O Sea, stern mother of
Thy tempests sing in me, thy billows
roll

Hjalmar H. Boyesen.

New York Ap. 26th 1888

HJALMAR HJORTH BOYESEN.

In a capital story by Hjalmar Hjorth Boyesen, called "A Norseman's Pilgrimage," there is a chapter headed "Retrospect;" and if any one wishes to learn something about the youth of the author, he cannot do better than read that, for I have good reason to know that it is autobiographical.

"Olaf Varberg was by birth a Norwegian. His childhood had been spent in the fjords of Norway, where the grand solemnity of nature had tended to foster a certain brooding disposition of mind. Every hill, every stone, and every tree was a monument of past heroism, or at least to his wakeful sense suggested some untold record of the Norseman's forgotten glory. Not a hundred steps from his home stood King Bele's venerable tomb; and on this very strand, where so often he had sat

pensively gazing down into the blue deep,
it was that Frithjof landed in the summer
nights, and hastened to those forbidden
meetings with his beloved in Balder's
grove; and not very far from the house
there was a huge birch which certainly
must have been centuries old. It grew
upon a green hillock which the boy fancied looked like a tomb. Here under this
tree he had spent perhaps the happiest
moments of his life. In the long, light
summer evenings, he would sit there for
hours listening to the strange, soft melo-
dies of the wind as it breathed through the
full-leafed crown.

" He felt sure that it was a scald who was
buried here; for in the songs of the wind
he had seemed to recognize the same
strain that had rung in his ears so often
while reading the scaldic lays in the old
sagas. Then strange emotions would thrill
through his breast; he felt that he was
himself a scald, and that he was destined
to revive the expiring song and the half-
forgotten traditions of the great old time.

" When he was twelve years old he had

himself written a long poem which he had entitled 'The Saga of the Scald.' He had only ventured to read it to his grandmother; but she had cried over it for a whole day, and that he felt to be a great reward."

Although all this is said of Olaf Varberg, the fictitious character, it is true of Hjalmar Hjorth Boyesen, as is much more in the same chapter; though his father was not killed in the war, but is still alive.

Mr. Boyesen was born on Sept. 23, 1848, at Fredricksvern, a small seaport on the southern coast of Norway. "Why cannot the Scandinavian Peninsula sail?" is an old conundrum; to which the answer is, "Because it was launched with the keel up." A huge granite ridge runs north and south, separating Norway from Sweden, with ribs of rock springing from it like the ribs of a ship. The sea flows in between the ribs, and the gulfs and bays thus shut in by the mountains are the fjords, amid the majestic scenery of which the boyhood of Mr. Boyesen was passed.

"How often," he says, "have I drifted through the spacious summer days in my

sharp-keeled wherry, upon those light, glittering waters, while the seabirds surged in
airy waves above me, and the white clouds
with a bewildering distinctness pursued
their tranquil paths far down in the deep
below! It gave one a feeling of being
suspended in the midst of the vast blue
space, hovering between two infinities; and
it seemed at the moment often hard to
determine whether the real heavens were
above or below. Then to watch the sub-
tile play of color, how the lucid green vies
with the feebler air-tints ; to listen with
luxurious listlessness to the musical plash-
ing of the water against the bow ; to follow
the placid soaring of the large, white-
breasted sea-gulls, as they float on broad,
motionless wings, through the viewless
ether ; and to feel all the while the vast
presence of the heaven-piercing peaks and
glaciers, like a huge, dim background,
upon which your sensations trace themselves in a deliciously vague and rich
relief, — ah ! it is the perfection of pure
and simple being, one of those moments
when the mere fact of living seems a great
and glorious thing."

"I remember how as a boy my whole being thrilled with the proud consciousness that I was a Norseman, a Goth of the pure old stock, a descendant of those daring Vikings who conquered Normandy and England, and who spread the terror of their name even to Italy and Constantinople."

His mother died while he was still young, and he was brought up by her father, Judge Hjorth of Systrand. His most pronounced trait at this period was his love of animals: he had several hundred pigeons, and besides these a lot of rabbits, dogs, cows, and even horses. All his pigeons were named after characters in the books he read, both historic and fictitious; and in his imagination they repeated the adventures ascribed to the originals.

There was an old tenant on the estate, named Gunnar, who took a great fancy to the boy, and initiated him into all the mysteries of wood-craft. He knew every sight and sound in the woods, and what they meant. Sometimes the boy spent entire nights with him in the woods, sleeping in the mountain chalêts or "saeters," in order

to be in time for the birds and beasts that
came to drink at the springs and lakes in
the mornings. As a result, his senses were
as alert as those of an Indian, and he was
a good shot and an expert fisherman.
Signs of the weather, the proper season of
the year and time of day for all kinds
of game, the best way of making flies for
trout, — such things as these were quite
familiar to the boy, who wandered through
the forests of spruce, fir, birch, and hem-
lock, on the steep slopes of the fjords, with
old Gunnar.

"I assure you," said Mr. Boyesen to me
one day, "that I have never since had so
keen an enjoyment of life as I had then.
I need only shut my eyes to see the clear
mountain tarns at sunrise, where the fish
leaped in the sun, or the dark rivers at
night where we went trout-fishing, and the
great splashes in the stream as the line
flew off the reel. By the way, have you
ever sat through the night at a lonely
river, and seen the otter go a-fishing? He
plumps so quietly into the stream, and you
see nothing but perhaps a little black

moving speck, and the gleam of his eyes, and his long whiskers."

It was a rule in Judge Hjorth's house, that the children should go to bed at nine o'clock ; but the servants' hall had an irresistible attraction for Hjalmar (whose name, and many other Norse names, will not be so difficult to pronounce, by the way, if the reader will remember that the *j* is sounded like the *y* in "yacht" and "Yankee.") Hjalmar loved to sit up, and listen to the rough peasant dialect of the servants as they sang ballads, and told stories of trolls and brownies, and the achievements of their ancestors. In spite of all prohibitions he could not keep away from this enchanted world ; and he confesses that often after having kissed his grandfather and grandmother "good night," he would steal down into the kitchen, and sit spell-bound, gazing and listening, until his disobedience was discovered, and he was ignominiously undressed and put to bed.

The day came for him to leave home to go to school in the city, but when his trunk had been packed, and the steamer was due,

he could not be found. Messengers were
sent hither and thither; they searched
every nook and corner, and shouted his
name, without getting any answer. The
household was distracted. The steamer
loomed up in the fjord, and slowly came to
the landing. Still the boy did not return.
He had been seen in the morning, on the
pier, and boats were sent out with dragnets
to search for him in the water. There was
no trace of him there. At last one of the
dairymaids suggested that he might have
gone to the pasture where the calves were
kept, to say good-by to the cattle ; and there,
sure enough, he was discovered, with his
arms around the neck of a calf, over which
he was weeping bitter tears. He had
started out to say farewell to all his pets
on the estate, and had been so overcome
with grief at having to leave this particular
calf, which had been given to him, that he
had forgotten all about the steamer, which
lay shrieking impatiently, and belching
forth smoke, in the fjord.

His incurable homesickness made his
school life miserable, although he was

amply able to hold his own with the other boys, who had a great respect for his knowledge of fishing and hunting and all those things that he had learned in his excursions with Gunnar. Those excursions, with all their sights and sounds, — the rainbow flicker of the trout, the ripples in the otter's wake, the music of the waterfalls, the calm twilight of the woods, the scent of the pines, — came back to him now in such vivid sensations that he could not apply himself to his books; but he had so much natural aptitude, that, though he rarely took up a lesson until it was within a few minutes of the time to recite it, he managed to keep about the middle of his class, and occasionally advanced towards the top on account of the literary ability of his compositions. These were the only exercises that interested him in the beginning, but the praise he received for them gradually aroused his ambition in other directions.

He was a plucky boy, and was not without some " noble scars." There was a feud of ancient standing between the boys of the Latin School and those who did not rejoice in a classical education, and a Latin-School boy who ventured upon hostile territory was sure to be pounced upon by the " plebs" and unmercifully beaten if he was not able to defend himself. Boyesen had no fear of these encounters, and often sought them, though he was now and then routed in the fortunes of war.

During the summer vacations he returned to his beautiful home on the Sognefjord, making the journey on foot, — a distance of nearly two hundred miles, — with a knapsack on his back, at a season of the year when the country was at its loveliest; and thus he was enabled to renew his acquaintance with peasant life, and to listen again to the legends that had charmed him in the servants' hall.

He did not like city life, or the ancient languages which he had to learn at school; and he sought relief in his compositions. He wrote the most blood-curdling tragedies and romances; and like Olaf Varberg, the hero of " A Norseman's Pilgrimage," he found an appreciative listener in his

grandmother. After seeing " Hamlet" for
the first time at the Christiania Theatre,
he wrote a play in which the hero was
killed in the first act and re-appeared as a
ghost in the remaining four acts: even thus
did his juvenile imagination parody Shakspeare's greatest work! But his talent was
genuine, and only needed direction and
development to rise above such imitative
efforts as these; though the only encouragement he received was from his grandmother.

"Norway is too small a country to
support poets," his father said. "If you
are serious in your aspirations to become
a man of letters," he added, "you ought
to conquer a language in which you can
address the great world, — English, French,
or German, — that is, if you have any thing
to say which the world will care to listen
to."

His father had a restless and ambitious
spirit, which rebelled against the slow and
conservative methods of Norway. He had
been to America, and he liked this country
better than his own, and thought that it

would be well for his sons if they would come here. He had even deposited a sum of money with a friend in Chicago, which was to be paid to any one of his sons who should appear to claim it in person.

Hjalmar himself was as eager to try his fortunes in the new country as his father was to have him; but Judge Hjorth violently opposed the idea at first, though afterwards, when the boy had taken his degree at the university, the old gentleman yielded to his persuasions. This was in 1868, when Hjalmar was only twenty years old ; and though his intention on starting out was to return to Norway in a year, he found the United States so attractive that he made this country his home.

For a time he was employed in editing a Scandinavian paper; then he became a teacher; and he acquired the language so rapidly, that at the end of two years he was able to write a book which is a model of racy and vigorous English. He was not without homesickness, and it was natural that in composing this book his thoughts should go back to the deep, mountain-

clasped fjords, and the high valleys, shel-
tered in which he had so often sat before
the peasant's fire listening to the legends
of the wonderful North-land. Gunnar came
back to his mind, and he gave that name to
his hero, though the latter had not at all
the character of the old woodman.

The originality and power of the book
were recognized at once: it was full of life
and motion, and gave one the sensation of
walking side by side with a vigorous companion, across some clear upland on an ex-
hilarating autumn morning. Here was an
author who had new stories to tell, and
who could tell them so well that the pulse
of the listener bounded in unison with his,
in watching the movements of his characters. Norway had given America a new
novelist.

Since then Mr. Boyesen has fortified his
position in literature by many delightful
books, all glowing with nervous vitality and
sparkling like the water in his native cas-
cades. So many of them are there, that
an ordinary writer might point to them
alone in proof of his industry; but their

production has been merely a recreation to him, and the greater part of his time is given to the duties of a professorship in Columbia College, New York.

How "Gunnar" found a publisher, he has told us as follows : —

"One day in July, 1871, I happened to be in the Harvard College Library, Cambridge. Professor Ezra Abbot, who was then assistant librarian, begged me to write my name in the visitors' book. He became interested in it, philologically. He asked about my nationality, and, hearing that I was a Norseman, begged leave to make me acquainted with Professor Child, who just then was in need of a Norseman.

" Professor Child was sent for and arrived. He gave me Landstadt's collection of Norwegian ballads, and begged me read and translate a number of passages which he had marked. He was then at work upon his great book on ballads, two volumes of which have now appeared. We spent the whole afternoon reading Norse ballads written in different dialects which were all familiar to me.

" When we parted, Professor Child exclaimed, ' You have a lot of valuable material in your possession. Why don't you make use of it? It would make an interesting article.'

" I replied that I had written something. He begged me to bring the MS. to him, and a few days later I was invited to dine at his house. Howells was

among the guests ; he was then editor of ' The Atlantic.'
After dinner I was requested to read a portion of my
MS. ; and I selected the chapter on the ' Skee Race,'
and, being asked for more, read the chapter entitled
' The Wedding of the Wild Duck.'

" Howells became greatly interested ; begged me to
spend a couple of days at his house as his guest, and
read the rest of the tale. This invitation was accepted,
and likewise the MS.

" It was this incident which had the most decisive
influence upon my life, as it was probably the cause
of my remaining in this country. I then became
acquainted with Mr. Longfellow, Mr. Lowell, Henry
James, Jr., and others. It changed the face of the
United States to me, and launched me fairly upon my
career as a man of letters."

THOMAS WENTWORTH HIGGINSON.

THE quaint old village, with its straggling houses, and deep shade and quietude, which Lowell pictures for us as the Cambridge of his youth, was the scene of the boyhood of Thomas Wentworth Higginson also; and he too, though four years the junior of Lowell, was among the eager boys who buzzed around the door of the wonderful barber's shop, described in " Fireside Travels," where tomahawks and weapons from the antipodes hung upon the wall, and a parrot harangued the spectators and the customers in a gibberish which the barber said was the Hottentot language.

He went to the same school as Lowell, and sat under the same frowning eye, though the poet, who, as he says, seemed " immeasurably ancient," had been transferred to college; and his earliest recollec-

There is no conceivable
beauty of blossom so beautiful
as words -- none so graceful,
none so perfumed.

From "The Procession of the
Flowers" in Outdoor Papers.

Thomas Wentworth Higginson

Cambridge. Mass.

tions are of the library in the gambrel-roofed house where Oliver Wendell Holmes was born, and where he was as much at home as in his father's house, which adjoined that celebrated dwelling.

He was born in an atmosphere of learning and literature ; the walls of the house seemed to be made of books, and when he looked out of the windows, the college buildings were visible to remind him of further learning still. If ever a boy could claim to belong to the " academic races," as Dr. Holmes calls the families whose names have appeared generation after generation on the college rolls, it was Thomas Wentworth Higginson, who came of a long line of Puritanic clergymen and scholars, and who was himself born at the head of a street called Professors' Row (now Kirkland Street) because all the houses were occupied by professors in the neighboring university, of which his own father was the steward or bursar. The society in which his parents moved was intellectual, and many of their visitors were famous, like Edward Everett the orator,

Judge Story, and Margaret Fuller. Even his nurse added something to the influence of the literary current into which he was plunged, for she was Rowena Pratt, the wife of the original of Longfellow's " Village Blacksmith."

It would have been easy to make such surroundings odious to a boy, for a diet of learning alone is quite as likely to excite repugnance as a diet of pudding. Books may be as darkening as prison-bars, and they may be as full of sunlight and enchanting hues as windows filled with cathedral glass ; the difference depends partly on the boy himself, and partly on the manner in which he is educated. Thomas Wentworth Higginson was a born scholar, however, and in the reminiscences of his youth, books are not associated with confinement and restraint, but with pleasures as keen as any he found in the playground; he never sighed to escape from them, but derived from them all the delights which they possess for the boy who loves them. Even his Latin text-book had charms for him, as he has shown us

in one of his many graceful essays. "I
remember the very day when the schoolmaster gave it to me," he says. "He
was that vigorous, rigorous, kind-hearted,
thorough - bred Englishman, W. W. It
was the beginning of a new school-year.
Lowell, and Story, and the other old boys,
who seemed so immeasurably ancient, had
been transferred to college, and last year's
youngest class was at length youngest but
one, and ready for the 'New Latin Tutor.'
Then W. W. called us to his desk, and
opening it, — I can hear the very rattle of
the birch, as it rolled back from the up-
lifted lid, — he brought out for us these
books, in all the glory of fresh calf binding,
and gave each volume into trembling boyish hands. To some of us there was more
of birch than of bounty in the immediate
associations of that desk ; and I fancy that
we always trembled a little when we had a
new book, as if all the proverbial floggings
which it might involve were already tin-
gling between its covers. Yet those of us
whose love of the book was wont to save
us from the rod, may have felt the thrill of

delight predominate; at any rate, there was
novelty, and the 'joy of eventful living,'
and I remember that the rather stern and
aquiline face of our teacher relaxed into
mildness for a moment. But we and our
books must have looked very fresh and
new to him, though we may all be a little
battered now; at least, my 'New Latin
Tutor' is. The change undergone by the
volume which Browning put in the plum-
tree cleft, to be read only by newts and
beetles, —

> "With all the binding all of a blister,
>   And great blue spots where the ink has run,
>   And reddish streaks that wink and glister," —

could hardly exceed what this book shows,
when I fish it up from a chest of literary
lumber coeval with itself. It would smell
musty, doubtless, to any nose unregulated
by a heart; but to me it is redolent of
the alder-blossoms of boyish springs, and
the aromatic walnut odor which used in
autumn to pervade the dells of 'Sweet
Auburn,' that lay not so very far from our
schoolhouse. It is a very precious book,

and it should be robed in choice Turkey morocco, were not the very covers too much a part of the association to be changed. For between them I gathered the seed-grain of many harvests of delight; through this low archway I first looked upon the immeasurable beauty of words."

In his own house there was a library rich in the literature of the age of Queen Anne; and when he was tired of reading himself, his mother read to him, while he stretched himself out on the hearth-rug and gazed into the fire. The library in the minister's house next door was open to him also, — that fascinating place which the "Autocrat of the Breakfast Table" (then a student of medicine) has described for us in both prose and verse; the old gambrel-roofed house, with the picture of Dorothy Q., and the marks of the redcoats' muskets on the floor.

The father of the "Autocrat" was fond of his neighbor's children, as well as of his own, and, without a murmur of complaint, allowed them to romp in his library among the books, which were as varied in their uniforms as the members of the Ancient and Honorable Artillery Company. Once, when the weather was cold, he joined them at the window where they stood admiring the traceries of frost on the panes; and, seeing the twinkling points of light among the crystals, he wrote underneath a motto which remained with them as though the words had been cut in their memories rather than in the vanishing frost, — *Per aspera ad astra*, — which they all knew meant " Through difficulties to the stars."

Though a bookish boy, Thomas Wentworth Higginson was as vigorous as any dunce ; but he was precocious, and though only thirteen years of age when he entered Harvard College, he looked much older. The studiousness of his earlier years was not abated now, and at a time when most boys are only freshmen, or at preparatory schools, he was graduated. Curiously enough he was fond of mathematics, which are usually the aversion of students of literary tastes ; but literature had the greatest charm for him, and during his college years a group of new authors came into prominence who had a lifelong influence upon him as upon the rest of the world. "Tennyson's thin early volumes were being handed about, and seemed to bring a richer coloring into the universe; Carlyle was talked of in the evening by my elder brothers; and one day the fresh wit and wisdom of · Pickwick' came to delight us all. . . . Emerson had often lectured at Cambridge, and his volume of essays had just appeared. This was given to me by my mother, and was read as I never had read any other book."

After his graduation, the young student said that he would like to be a blacksmith, — thinking that by working at the forge and anvil he could learn how to sympathize with that great division of mankind which such as he usually know only through books; but he was dissuaded from this, and became a teacher, a preacher, and an author. Perhaps it is as an author that he is most distinguished now, but we ought not to forget, in enumerating his accomplishments, that " Colonel " is not a brevet honor in his case, and that it was honorably acquired in the Civil War when he commanded a black regiment.

CHARLES DUDLEY WARNER.

" One of the best things in the world is to be a boy. It requires no experience, though it needs some practice to be a good one. The disadvantage of the position is that it does not last long enough; it is soon over. Just as soon as you get used to being a boy, you have to be something else, with a good deal more work to do, and not half so much fun."

This is said by Charles Dudley Warner, in a delightful little volume called " Being a Boy," the copy of which that lies before me, borrowed from the public library, bears on its titlepage the pencilled comments of two previous readers, in schoolboy hand : " Putty gud book," " Rawther Sawcastick."

It is a " putty gud book," and it is " rawther sawcastick ; " it leaves nothing unsaid that is worth knowing about the life of a boy on a New-England farm, and it is as

The Son of an Emir had red hair of which he was ashamed, and wished to dye it. Nay, my son, said the Emir, rather so behave that all fathers shall wish their sons had red hair

Chas Dudley Warner

April 6 1877.

natural and as shyly humorous as Aldrich's history of Tom Bailey at Rivermouth. No doubt those who have read it, or who may read it in the future, will be glad to know that it is in a measure autobiographical; that in writing it, Mr. Warner sat for his own portrait, and painted what he saw in the looking-glass.

He was born on Sept. 12, 1827, in Plainfield, Mass., a hilly town in the western part of the State, where his father had a farm of about six hundred acres, with large flocks of sheep and herds of cattle; and his boyhood was like that of the typical farmer's boy who appears in his book, though in his case the labor and the trials were sweetened by a love of Nature, which gathered something more than physical enjoyment from his surroundings.

The summer soon passed away, and the winters seemed to be never-ending on that lofty plateau. The snows drifted high above the fences, and sleighs could go anywhere over the fields. The winds blew strong; and once, when Charles Dudley Warner started across the solid shining crust of the snow for the schoolhouse that was about half a mile away, with his dinner-basket in his hand, and a red cloak drawn around him, the tempest reversed the fable, and snatched both basket and cloak away from him, carrying them off into the forest, where they were not recovered until the following spring.

He hated cold, and says now that the so-called invigorating climate of New England fills the graveyard with young tenants; but sometimes he could forget it, as when, having an apple to eat, he came home from school on a bitter day without noticing that the flaps of his cap were loose, and that his ears were frozen.

The house was an old-fashioned place, with rambling woodsheds and out-buildings, and a big kitchen. There were no stoves, but great cavernous fireplaces, hedged in by settles, the backs of which protected the family from draughts when they sat before the blazing fire. One curious article of furniture was a round table with a seat *under* it, and when the top was swung back it formed another settle.

A glorious place this kitchen was on a winter's evening. Stories were told, and songs sung, and it was the scene of Whittier's " Snow-bound " over again.

> " Between the andiron's straddling feet,
> The mug of cider simmered slow,
> The apples sputtered in a row,
> And close at hand the basket stood
> With nuts from brown October's wood."

And in addition to the cider, the nuts, and the apples, there were dishes of toasted cheese of a particular kind called "white oak," which was made from skimmed milk, and which would toast without melting. An enormous cellar was underneath the kitchen, full of cider-barrels, vegetables, and apples, which grew in abundance on the farm.

The principal events of the year were the cider-making in the fall, and the sugar-making in the spring. There were fine groves of sugar-maples on the farm; and in March or April, when the skies began to have a soft look and the steely light of winter to grow more like gold, when there was a constant drip, drip, drip, from the eaves, and the elbows of the rocks showed through the white garment that was slipping away from them, the trees were tapped, and the buckets hung from them to catch the oozing sap. A camp was established in the woods, and all the family would be there for the "sugaring-off," which was done in the primitive way, with a big fire between two logs and the caldrons hung from a pole above. They make sugar now in brick houses, with elaborate apparatus; but, though the product is said to be improved, it is not half as sweet as it was at the old-fashioned "sugaring-off" with the logs blazing in the woods and the merry-making of former days, — the days of fifty years ago when Charles Dudley Warner was a boy.

Of course he knew something about traps, and trapping too; and he was devoted to the "hired man" who taught him how to make and use various kinds of snares. He used to go to bed and get up with this man, and help him to build the great fire, first raking the embers and then piling the sticks high up: it used to take a quarter of a cord of wood to build that fire.

Oh the winters, the everlasting winters! Often the snow would be heaped up in drifts higher than the windows, and a permanent tunnel had to be made from the house to the barn. The cellar was as dark as midnight, for tan-bark was banked all around the house to keep out the besieging cold.

Occasionally his father took him on journeys: once to the Connecticut River, and he craned his neck out of the window to see Sugar Loaf Mountain. It was in vain, for all the hills were more or less round and green, and there was not one that looked at all like the conical loaf of sugar which they had at home. And then his grandfather took him to the city, not New York City, or Boston, or any large city, but to Hudson; which, small as it was, struck him as no other place has ever done since. The fruit-stalls are remembered more vividly than any thing else, and a man at one of the stalls offered to trade an orange for all the buttons on his coat ; he was afraid of that man.

Though active, he was an imaginative and a dreamy boy, and his fancy transformed the common sights of the woods and fields to objects of chivalry and romance as he leaped from rock to rock in the high pastures ; he was not afraid of being alone, though there seemed to be strange voices in the trees.

When he was five years old he lost his father, who, though not a college-bred man, was fond of reading, and owned the largest library in the town excepting the minister's ; and then he was sent to live with a relative at Charlemont, nine miles from Plainfield, where he attended the district school. It is Charlemont that is described in " Being a Boy."

He was a pretty fair scholar, but the " chores " took most of his time, and books were scarce. Had he been able to choose, he would have entered on a military career. But when he was about twelve he went to live at Cazenovia, N.Y., and there his literary tastes were encouraged by access to the books for which he had been starving. He was a clever hand at composition, and took Washington Irving as a model. His guardian intended him for trade, however; and for a time he was employed in a drug-shop, and then in the post-office. Afterwards he entered Hamilton College, from which he was graduated in 1851. He filled reams of paper with rhymes, essays, and romances, and was always active in the debating society. But he had no idea of becoming a professional author. Having given up his military aspirations, he turned his eyes towards public life; speech-making seemed to be a great accomplishment, and a Congressman a star of considerable magnitude. This dream of glory was not fulfilled; his health was poor after his graduation, and in order to restore it he went to Missouri with a party of surveyors. After this adventure he studied law, and practised a little in Chicago; but at last (though not until he was thirty-one) he took up journalism as a profession, and eventually, like Howells and Stedman, branched out in the direction of more permanent literature.

His books sometimes remind us of Holmes by their philosophical playfulness; of Lamb by the quaintness of their humor; of Irving by their placidity; and of Steele or Addison by the purity of their style. They have a surface of smiles, but under the smiles are the deep thoughts of an earnest nature.

Vailima
Jan 2? 1894

Dear Mr Rideing,

    I shall have much pleasure in trying to write what you want — or truely. about five items and words (probably of reminiscences).

~~[illegible crossed-out line]~~

        Yours faithfully
        Robert Louis Stevenson

William H. Rideing Esq.

ROBERT LOUIS STEVENSON.

If there is any boy who has not yet read " Treasure Island " and " Kidnapped," he may be pitied in one sense and envied in another sense; for though he has lost much, he has much to gain, — he has joys before him which others have already known. Of all modern books that a boy should rejoice in, there is none comparable with those two, both of them equal in a way to "Robinson Crusoe," and both, like Defoe's masterpiece, so permanent as works of art that they can never be outgrown.

A boy who cares for reading at all usually reads everything he can reach; but if he is a healthy boy, and has any choice, he soon shows his preference for romance. He will give up Bunyan for Scott, Miss Edgeworth for Marryat, and a bushel of moral tales for a handful of stirring adventures.

Through the magic of a hint of a buccaneer, such a boy will snap his teeth upon an imaginary cutlass, and slap his hip in search of an unsubstantial pistol; see himself (much larger than life) parading coral beaches, or lolling under crimson sails in the midday heat of tropical reefs, or under the mild light of the southern stars, — a fire-eater, a dare-devil, an exploiter of untold riches; in turn, a Drake, a Frobisher, or a Magellan.

But let him return to the mass of such fiction when he has grown older, and the sadness of experience has clipped his wings, as it were. What rubbish most of it seems; and how he will yawn over the narratives that once transported him, now to the ice-bound ship in the clutch of the Arctic, then to the pampas, now to the African lakes, and then to the Indian jungle! The lights have gone out on that wonderful panorama in which icebergs, palms, and banyans had life and movement, and all the beasts of the ark swung in a fascinating rotation.

But though other books fade, "Robin-

son Crusoe" keeps as fresh as ever for the
boys of these days as it was for the boys
who saw Defoe in Fleet Street when
William the Third was king; and not for
boys alone, but also for graybeards.

So it is with Stevenson's stories of adventure. One can never be too old to lose
interest in David Balfour or Alan Breck
Stewart, and never fail to smell the heather
and the brine in all their exciting experiences by sea and by land.

Defoe wrote other books besides " Robinson Crusoe," and was the author of some
virulent pamphlets which led him to the
pillory; but how many boys think of him
except for that one-story ? Stevenson has
written essays and poems which show his
genius as clearly as his fiction ; but there
is a possibility that posterity will remember
him more gratefully for "Treasure Island"
and " Kidnapped " than for anything else.

He was not at all shy in describing himself. Indeed, few authors of equal rank
and permanence ever confided so much as
he did to his readers. He held himself up
as a mirror in which they might see them-

selves ; he lets us into all his little secrets, and yet discloses nothing ignoble, nothing that does not create sympathy, and amuse or elevate. By reading his " Memories and Portraits," one might take the story of his youth from his own lips, as it were, and that revelation only needs the confirmation of a few friends, which it already has.

He was born in Edinburgh in 1850, and came of a family distinguished as inventors and engineers. Mariners, who sail the stormy and rock-bound seas of Scotland, have reason to be grateful to the Stevensons; for the grandfather, father, and uncles of Robert Louis designed and superintended the erection of the lighthouses that now beam on many of the most fearsome reefs and headlands on the coast. Robert himself was intended by his parents to be an engineer, and to pursue the family calling; but he was not that sort of a boy. He could not learn by rote what other boys learnt ; he was delicate, dreamy, unpractical — a reader, but not a scholar.

There is very little doubt that he caused

his father and mother much anxiety and some disappointment. " From my earliest childhood," he says, " it was mine to make a plaything of imaginary events ; and as soon as I was able to write I became a good friend to the paper-makers." He scribbled and read a great deal, and, instead of going to school, explored the hills and glens of the Pentlands, until there was hardly a rivulet that he did not know, from its source to the sea; and in all his rambles one may be sure his mind was full of the imaginings which are fed by the romantic past and aspect of such a country as Scotland. " A Scottish child," he says, " hears much of shipwreck, outlying iron skerries, pitiless breakers, and great sea-lights ; much of heathery mountains, wild clans, and hunted Covenanters. Breaths come to him in song of the distant Cheviots, and the ring of foraying hoofs. He glories in his hard-fisted forefathers, of the iron girdle and the handful of oatmeal, who rode so swiftly and lived so sparsely on their raids."

Sometimes he was taken by his father or his uncles on their expeditions to the wild islands and headlands where they were building lighthouses; and thus he made the acquaintance of the island of Earraid, on which David Balfour was wrecked in the brig " Covenant."

" Fifteen miles away to seaward a certain black rock stood environed by the Atlantic rollers, the outpost of the Torran reefs. Here was a tower to be built, and a star lighted for the conduct of seamen. But as the rock was small, and hard of access, and far from the land, the work would be one of years; and my father was now looking for a shore station where the stones might be quarried and dressed, the men live, and the tender, with some degree of safety, lie at anchor. . . . Here was no living presence save for the limpets on the rocks, for some old, gray, rain-beaten ram that I might rouse out of a ferny den betwixt two bowlders, or for the haunting and piping of the gulls. It was older than man ; it was found so by incoming Celts and seafaring Norsemen and Columba's priests. The earthy savor of the bog-plants; the rude disorder of the bowlders;

the inimitable seaside brightness of the air, the brine, and the iodine; the lap of the billows among the weedy reefs; the sudden springing-up of a great run of dashing surf along the sea-front of the isle, — all that I saw and felt my predecessors must have seen and felt with scarce a difference."

To say that he was idle is less true than to say that he revolted against discipline and ordinary lessons, though we find him frequently bewailing his own indolence. He describes himself as being, when he entered the University, a "lean, idle, unpopular student . . . whose changing humors, fine occasional purposes of good, flinching acceptance of evil, shiverings on wet, east-windy, morning journeys up to class, infinite yawnings during lecture, and unquenchable gusto in the delights of truancy, made up the sunshine and shadow of college life."

When he presented himself for a certificate in the engineering class, Professor Fleming Jenkin, whose life he afterwards wrote, said, "It is quite useless for *you* to come, Mr. Stevenson. There may be doubtful cases: there is no doubt about yours. You have simply *not* attended my class."

He was odd in dress, and odd in manner. A friend (Miss Eva Blantyre Simpson) who knew him in his college days says, "He wore the same dress on all occasions, — a shabby, short, velveteen jacket, a loose, Byronic-collared shirt, and meagre, shabby-looking trousers. His straight hair he wore long; and he looked like an unsuccessful artist, or a poorly clad but eager student.

"We teased him unmercifully for his peculiarities in dress and manner," says Miss Simpson. "It did not become a youth of his years, we held, to affect a bizarre style; and he held he lived in a free country, and could exercise his own taste at will. Nothing annoyed him more than to affirm his shabby clothes, his long cloak, which he wore instead of an orthodox great-coat, were eccentricities of genius. He certainly liked to be noticed, for he was full of the self-absorbed conceit of youth.

If he was not the central figure, he took what we called Stevensonian ways of attracting notice to himself. He would spring up full of a novel notion he had to expound (and his brain teemed with them), or he vowed he could not speak trammelled by a coat, and asked leave to talk in his shirt-sleeves. For all these mannerisms he had to stand a good deal of chaff, which he never resented, though he vehemently defended himself, or fell squashed for a brief space in a limp mass into a veritable back seat."

Without thirsting for academic honors, he took his degree at the University, and in obedience to his father's wishes joined the Scottish bar. For some time " R. L. Stevenson, Advocate," was on the door-plate of 17 Heriot Row, Edinburgh; but he never practised. He had no more inclination towards law than towards engineering: he loved the skies, he loved the moor, he loved to observe his fellow-men. There was everything in him to show to anybody who could understand that he was born for literature, and saturated with literature.

While he was apparently dreaming by the rills of the Pentland Hills, he was dipping into Spenser's "well of English undefiled," into the crystal springs of the best of literature. The reader knows, of course, that when Spenser spoke of this "well of English undefiled," he spoke of the style of Chaucer. In some other ways Stevenson reminds us of that poet. There was no game that had such an attraction for him as his books; and there were no books that could keep him in-doors, and make a pedant of him to the exclusion of his interest in nature.

An idler? When his teachers reproached him, and his parents had misgivings, he was quietly cultivating the art on which his mind was set, and cultivating it by a method which, frankly confessed by him, may be studied with the same advantage, though it has its defects, by all who hope to find the best expression for their thought.

Listen to this from his essay on "A College Magazine." "All through my boyhood and youth I was known and pointed out for the pattern of an idler; and yet I was

always busy on my own private end, which
was to learn to write. I kept always two
books in my pocket, one to read, one to
write in. As I walked, my mind was busy
fitting what I saw with appropriate words;
when I sat by the roadside, I would either
read, or a pencil and a penny version-book
would be in my hand, to note down the
features of the scene, or commemorate
some halting stanzas. . . . It was not
so much that I wished to be an author
(though I wished that too) as I had vowed
that I would learn to write. . . . Whenever I read a book or a passage that particularly pleased me, in which a thing was
said or an effect rendered with propriety,
in which there was either some conspicu-
ous force or some happy distinction in the
style, I must sit down myself and ape that
quality. I was unsuccessful, and I knew it,
and tried again, and was again unsuccessful! but at least, in these vain bouts I got
some practice in rhythm, in harmony, in
construction, and the co-ordination of parts.
I have thus played the sedulous ape to
Hazlitt, to Lowell, to Wordsworth, to Sir

Thomas Browne, to Defoe, to Hawthorne, to Montaigne, to Baudelaire, and to Obermann. . . . Even at the age of thirteen I had tried to do justice to the inhabitants of the famous city of Peebles in the style of the 'Book of Snobs.' . . . But enough has been said to show by what arts of impersonation and what puny ventriloquial effects I first saw my words on paper. . . . It was so Keats learned, and there never was a finer temperament for literature than Keats's."

I should like to quote more of this essay — not to quote it, but to reproduce it from beginning to end ; but there is not space here. Whoever desires a lesson in the art of writing English can have it gratuitously in the pages of " Memories and Portraits."

Enough has been said, however, to show that when he seemed to be idling, Stevenson was serving, in a quiet, undemonstrative way, his apprenticeship to the profession of literature; and though popular recognition did not come until he was over thirty, when, strange to say, it was the

brilliance of a story written for boys
("Treasure Island") which opened the
eyes of readers who had failed to see his
genius in earlier and profounder writing, he
lived long enough, brief as his years were,
to find himself celebrated, and perhaps
immortal — *perhaps* immortal as one who
uses words with a sense of their true value,
certainly immortal for a keen sense of the
noblest things in life, and a constant aspiration towards heaven.

He was busy to the last, brave to the
last, gay to the last; though his thoughts
(not all confessed) wandered back lovingly
from the pleasant natives and the perennial
foliage of the tropics to the crags and gray
mist of his native Edinburgh. Two things
should be borne in mind about him : as a
famous French critic said of another author,
he put a book into a page, a page into a
phrase, a phrase into a word, a thought
into a single image. This is true of his
work. Of his personality we may say that
he resembled in many ways his hero, Alan
Breck Stewart; and like him he might have
cried, "O man ! am I no a bonny fighter."

VERY different in most respects were Robert Louis Stevenson and Rudyard Kipling. Unlike Stevenson, Kipling was gay, not moody; active, not contemplative; vigorous, not delicate; an enthusiast in all boyish games, a lover of mischief, and the boon companion of the rough-and-tumble, hard-fisted, hard-headed boys who filled a military school in Devonshire.

The one thing in which they were closely akin was their delight in the military and naval prowess of their native lands, and their passion for the ballads and stories which recount the deeds of valor done by the great soldiers and mariners of British history.

Otherwise one cannot conceive a greater contrast than that between the lank, over-grown, queerly dressed school-boy of Edinburgh, who haunted churchyards, and

Jan. 7. 94.

Dear Mr Ridewig
I send with this
typed copy of the Indian Railway
tale – The Bold 'Prentice I think
it comes under your length limit
If it does not I can have it
down if you will return it.
Please let me have a look at it
in slip-proof
Very sincerely yours
Rudyard Kipling.

hatched melancholy thoughts in them like
a young Hamlet, and the small, lithe, mischievous, prankish youth, who had been
sent back to England by his parents in
India for education in an academy filled
by the sons of officers in the army and
navy, and who relished the Spartan life he
had to lead.

Kipling is usually reticent, very reticent,
about himself (and in that, too, he is unlike his contemporary, who, as we know
very well, poured out his confidences like
a friendly child) ; but he has described his
life at the school in "The Youth's Companion" in a rare chapter of autobiography,
from which we may quote.

The United Service College, as it was
called, was on the shores of Bristol Chan-
nel, near a little place known as Westward
Ho, so named after Rev. Charles Kingsley's
famous story, the scene of which is laid
in the days of Queen Elizabeth, when the
safety of England was threatened by the
Spanish Armada. Sir Walter Raleigh, Sir
Richard Grenville, Admiral Hawkins, and
Sir Francis Drake appear in the story ; and

the reader who loves romance can imagine what visions of adventure must have come to a boy who found himself living amidst such association.

The college " stood within two miles of Amyas Leigh's house at Northam, overlooking the Burroughs and the Pebble-ridge, and the mouth of the Torridge, whence the ' Rose ' sailed in search of Don Guzman. From the front dormitory windows, across the long rollers of the Atlantic, you could see Lundy Island and the Shutter Rock, where the ' Santa Catherina' galleon cheated Amyas out of his vengeance by going ashore. Inland lay the rich Devonshire lanes and the fat orchards ; and to the west the gorse and the turf rose and fell along the tops of the cliffs in combe after combe, till you came to Clovelly and the Hobby and Gallantry Bower, and the homes of the Carews and the Pinecoffins, and the Devonshire people that were old when the Armada was new."

A milksop, a boy without spirit, a boy without a vigorous constitution, could not have been happy in such a school, and, indeed, he would have been entirely out of place. The discipline was severe, as exercised by the masters and by the students themselves, who never forgot that they were preparing themselves to be soldiers.

"The school motto," says Kipling, "was, ' Fear God, Honour the King ; ' and so the men she made went out to Boerland and Zululand, and India and Burma, and Cyprus and Hongkong, and lived or died as gentlemen and officers.

" Even the most notorious bully, for whom an awful ending was prophesied, went to Canada, and was mixed up in Riel's rebellion, and came out of it with a fascinating reputation of having led a forlorn hope, and behaved like a hero. The first officer killed in the last Burma war was one of our boys, and the school was well pleased to think it should be so.

" All these matters were noted by the older boys; and when their fathers, the gray-whiskered colonels and generals, came down to see them, or the directors, who were K. C. B's., and had been desperate, hard-fighting men in their time, made a tour of inspection, it was reported that the school-tone was 'healthy.' This meant that the boys were straining on their leashes, and that there was a steady clatter of singlesticks and clinking of foils in the gymnasium at the far end of the corridor, where the drill-sergeant was barking out the regulation cuts and guards."

They were great swimmers, and there was not a single boy who could not do his quarter of a mile. The links at Westward Ho are considered among the best in England, and the boys played golf long before it became fashionable.

"We were weak in cricket; but our football team at its best devastated the country from Blundell's [1] — we always respected Blundell's, because 'Great John Ridd' had been educated there — to Exeter, whose team were grown men. Yet we, who had been taught to play together, drove them back over the November mud, back to their own goal-posts, till the ball was hacked through and touched down,

---

[1] Blundell's is the old school at Tiverton which John Ridd, the hero of "Lorna Doone," attended.

and you could hear the long-drawn yell of
' Schoo-*ool !* Schoo-*ool !* ' as far as Apple-
dore.

" When the enemy would not come to
us, our team went to the enemy, and if
victorious, would return late at night in
a three-horse brake chanting : —

> ' It's a way we have in the Army,
>   It's a way we have in the Navy,
> It's a way that we have in the Public Schools,
>   Which nobody can deny ! '

" Then the boys would flock to the dormitory windows, and wave towels, and join in
the ' Hip-hip-hip-hurrah ! ' of the chorus ;
and the winning team would swagger
through the dormitories, and show the
beautiful blue marks on their shins, and the
little boys would be allowed to get sponges
and hot water."

There was a school paper ; and Kipling
tells us of that also in his characteristic
style : —

" Three of the boys, who had moved up
the school side by side for four years, and
were allies in all things, started the notion

as soon as they came to the dignity of a study of their own with a door that would lock. The other two told the third boy what to write, and held the staircase against invaders.

" It was a real printed paper of eight pages ; and at first the printer was more thoroughly ignorant of type-setting, and the editor was more completely ignorant of proof-reading, than any printer and any editor that ever was. It was printed off by a gas-engine, and even the engine despised its work ; for one day it went through the floor of the shop, and crashed — still working furiously — into the cellar.

"The paper came out at times and seasons ; but every time it came out there was sure to be trouble, because the editor was learning for the first time how sweet and good and profitable it is — and how nice it looks on the page — to make fun of people in actual print.

" For instance, there was friction among the study-fags once ; and the editor wrote a descriptive account of the lower school, — the classes whence the fags were drawn,

— their manners and customs, their ways of cooking half-plucked sparrows and imperfectly cleaned blackbirds at the gas-jets on a rusty nib, and their fights over sloe-jam made in a gallipot. It was an absolutely truthful article ; but the lower school knew nothing about truth, and would not even consider it as literature.

"It is less safe to write a study of an entire class than to discuss individuals one by one ; but apart from the fact that boys throw books and inkpots very straight indeed, there is surprisingly little difference between the abuse of grown-up people and the abuse of children.

" In those days the editor had not learned this ; so when the study below the editorial study threw coal at the editorial legs, and kicked in the panels of the door, because of personal paragraphs in the last number, the editorial staff — and there never was so loyal and hard-fighting a staff — fried fat bacon till there was half an inch of grease in the pan, and let the greasy chunks down at the end of a string to bob against and defile the lower study windows.

"When the lower study — and there never was a public so low and unsympathetic as that lower study — looked out to see what was frosting their window-panes, the editorial staff emptied the hot fat on their heads, and it stayed there for days and days, wearing shiny to the very last."

It is not avowed that Kipling was the editor of that paper, but I think he was. The incident of the bacon certainly seems to fit him.

When they left school, most of the boys entered the army; but for some reason not explained Kipling did not do so. He returned to his family in India, and became, at the age of nineteen, a reporter, editor, and war correspondent of an Anglo-Indian newspaper.

The trying conditions under which his work was done, he himself has described : —

"The paper began running the last issue of the week on Saturday night, which is to say Sunday morning, after the custom of a London paper. This was a great convenience ; for immediately after the paper was put to bed, the dawn would lower the

thermometer from 96 to almost 84 for half
an hour; and in that chill — you have no
idea how cold is 84 on the grass until you
begin to pray for it — a very tired man
could set off to sleep ere the heat aroused
him.

"One Saturday night it was my pleasant
duty to put the paper to bed alone. A
king or courtier or a community was going to die, or get a new constitution, or
do something that was important, on the
other side of the world; and the paper
was to be held open till the latest possible
minute in order to catch the telegram. It
was a pitchy black night, as stifling as a
June night can be; and the *loo*, the red-
hot wind from the westward, was booming
among the tinder-dry trees, and pretend-
ing that the rain was on its heels. Now
and again a spot of almost boiling water
would fall on the dust with the flop of a
frog, but all our weary world knew that
was only pretence. It was a shade cooler
in the press-room than the office; so I sat
there, while the type ticked and clicked,
and the night jars hooted at the windows,

and the all but naked compositors wiped the sweat from their foreheads, and called for water. The thing that was keeping us back, whatever it was, would not come off, though the *loo* dropped, and the last type was set, and the whole round earth stood still in the choking heat, with its finger on its lip, to wait the event. I drowsed, and wondered whether the telegraph was a blessing, and whether this dying man, or struggling people, was aware of the inconvenience the delay was causing. There was no special reason beyond the heat and worry to make tension; but as the clock-hands crept up to three o'clock, and the machines spun their fly-wheels two and three times to see that all was in order before I said the word that would set them off, I could have shrieked aloud. Then the roar and rattle of the wheels shivered the quiet into little bits."

His daily work was to prepare for press all the telegrams of the day; to provide all the extracts and paragraphs; to make headed articles out of official reports, etc.; to write such editorial notes as he might have time for ; to look generally after all sports, out-station and local intelligence, and to read all proofs.

Hard as the work in the office was, he found time to write verses and stories of his own. Others could see all there was to see in that mixed life of British India. This young man, however, could not only see, but depict, and depict as no one else had done the redcoats and the natives and the governing classes. He had failed to enter the army; but he taught himself the speech, the ways, and the thoughts of the men in the ranks (remember his " Soldiers Three "), and of the commissioned officers, from the young lieutenant up to the commander-in-chief. Before he was twenty-five he found himself famous, and not only famous, but unique in qualities of observation and style among British authors.

www.ingramcontent.com/pod-product-compliance
Lightning Source LLC
Chambersburg PA
CBHW020057030726
47498CB00006B/1831